A Novel

THE GIRL WHO STOLE MY CHAIR!

By Thadeus Parkland

CHAPTER 1

Kimberlee's memories of her birth mother were nonexistent. The only woman she would ever know as 'mother' was the kind-hearted female who raised her; her maternal grandmother, Lydia Murrel. From a very young age, Lee was made aware her birth mother had left her to be raised by this unassuming woman in her mid-fifties. When Kimberlee sought answers, Lydia always told her what she wanted to know, with one exception. The only question she would never answer was the name of the woman who left Kimberlee to be raised by this woman in her late stage of life. Lydia's standard response was, "The girl who bore you did not want to have children. She and I agreed you would have a better life with me."

Lydia made a promise to herself to love and care for this child no matter what the future brought. She often questioned if this was the right choice for the two of them, especially when Kimberlee asked the woman she called mother why her birth mother never wanted her. Lydia responded with a pragmatic and straightforward answer: "The young girl was selfish and only wanted what would benefit her." Kimberlee hoped she would not ever be like her birth mother.

Kimberlee had few memories of a white girl living in the home she was reared in, a sister of sorts named Blanch. The vague recollections of the girl she adored when she was a toddler faded by the time she was ready to start preschool. Her sister left home without cause or reason, as best Kimberlee knew. The one memory that would stay with her for the rest of her life was her sister leaving without saying goodbye to her. Kimberlee didn't know why this memory was important to her as the teenage girl spent her time focused on herself and had little to do with the young girl.

When friends would visit, which was rare, the toddler was banished to her bedroom and was never allowed to join the older children. The exclusion from Blanch created a sense in Kimberlee that she did not belong. Her assumption was that Blanch was embarrassed by her appearance; her skin tone was much darker than her mother's or her sister's. For as long as she had been able to understand what people said, the color of her skin had always been a point of discussion.

Kimberlee had everything she needed but very little of what she wanted. At her young age, she didn't really understand why she was so different from everyone around her. She was the only child in her school with a dark complexion. People in the little town of Palestine, Texas, accepted Lydia's tale regarding the young girl's skin tone; "As a member of the Cherokee nation, my bloodline gave Kimberlee the deep coloring of her ancestors. Isn't she lucky?" Lydia willingly accepted the stares and whispers from the women in the small town. She thought it best to be chastised for being an unwed mother at her late age rather than for people to know the truth about Kimberlee's birth mother. Both she and Kimberlee were blessed with long straight flaxen hair; this attribute minimized the notion the young girl might be of a different race.

Lydia Murrel was fully aware that in this small East Texas town in 1965, if people had known Kimberlee's father was Afro-Latino and delivered by a 15-year-old white girl, a scandal would have ensued. It was painful enough to hear people question how a woman in her fifties and unmarried produced this child; it would have been far worse had the truth been revealed. Lydia opted to keep the Native American-Indian narrative as the explanation. Her silence around the topic left most to believe she had been raped and chose to keep the child, an act she was commended for behind closed doors. Lydia sensed that life for Kimberlee would have its challenges; this simple white lie kept one issue at bay.

She struggled emotionally knowing her own daughter rejected this beautiful child. The constant guilt she carried wore on her, creating a large amount of angst in her. The outcome of this emotion caused her to dote on Kimberlee from dawn to dusk in hopes the young girl would find her purpose in life and, ultimately, happiness.

The method of child-rearing was indeed a mistake, as whatever Lydia did, the young girl rarely appreciated it. Kimberlee appeared to always be seeking more of everything. Her grandmother, nay her mother, failed to understand what Kimberlee most needed was to find where she belonged. The hole left in her heart from being abandoned at birth appeared as if it would never heal.

Having worked outside the home since she was fourteen, Lydia was now fifty-four and beginning to slow down. From a very young age, her life was filled with endless challenges she fought to overcome. The home she grew up in was full of love and hard work but was not without its issues. Her father and mother raised her as an only child after the death of her older brother, who succumbed to the Spanish Flu. Physically unable to perform the chores her brother did on the farm, Lydia began working as a maid in the nearby town to offset the cost of the farmhands who assisted her father. She was steadfast in focusing on family and doing the right thing for those she loved. Even though offers of marriage occurred,

Lydia chose to help her family with their farm. After her father decided to sell a large parcel of their land and take life easy, Lydia decided she would accept a marriage proposal from a man who had recently moved to East Texas. The man she wed assumed Lydia's family was of means and would provide for him and his wife. When Lydia realized her new husband was a drunk who did nothing more than provide small doses of companionship to her, she began looking for a way out of the marriage. Three months after Blanch was born, her wish was granted.

Blanch's father packed his things and left the two women to fend for themselves. Lydia was not prepared for, nor did she expect to raise a child on her own in her late thirties, but with her husband gone, she and her family did the best they could to raise the young girl. Working, raising a daughter, and tending to her parents took its toll on Lydia. By the time her daughter was pregnant out of wedlock, Lydia was exhausted.

Knowing the hardships of being a single parent, Lydia didn't want her child to endure the difficulties she had. Devising a plan to reduce the challenges for her daughter took an unexpected turn when Blanch announced she did not want the child and was seeking options to dispose of it. This declaration by Blanch brought the trials and tribulations of dealing with her to the point of no return for Lydia.

Coming to an agreement to keep the child, before Blanch began to show, she went to stay with her recently widowed grandmother in the Texas countryside. The explanation to all who questioned this abrupt change was simple; Blanch would help her grandmother run the farm now that her grandfather was gone. Lydia never tried to persuade her daughter to raise her offspring; she knew the child would suffer at the hands of her selfish daughter. The night Kimberlee was born, it became apparent Blanch's desire not to acknowledge her baby was for the best. As planned, Blanch delivered Kimberlee at the farmhouse where her grandmother lived, far away from town.

When the trio returned to their home in Palestine, Texas, no signs were present Blanch had ever carried a child. Kimberlee came into the world far away from prying eyes. Lydia would raise Kimberlee as her own. Blanch's little sister would be cared for while Blanch focused on her schooling. Even with rumors of the child's origins running amuck, no one ever suspected Blanch of being the mother. The child, with its dark skin and black hair, could not possibly belong to the pale-skinned, blonde-haired Blanch.

The arrangement was ideal for Blanch; her mother, busy with the baby, permitted her to focus entirely on what she wanted. Blanch's entire purpose for living became focused on how to provide for herself. She wasn't afraid of hard work and was certainly not opposed to doing whatever it took to get what she desired. Every decision she made from the moment the child was born included a means to an end. Self-focus to the point of being a sociopath.

Lydia often quoted the tenth commandment in the Christian bible to Blanch, "Thou shalt not covet thy neighbor's ass." Even with the commanding nature of her mother's voice, Blanch had little concern for what the directive meant; she would ignore the lessons to be learned and spend her life pursuing the next best thing.

As Kimberlee grew, life around the Murrel household was reasonably calm. Blanch focused on school and working towards graduation; she had plans for college immediately after high school. With the recent event she had participated in on her grandmother's farm, she doubled down on her studies to ensure she was accepted to the university of her choosing.

While Blanch focused on her studies, Kimberlee developed into a nosey toddler who was very self-sufficient. While Lydia continued to work outside the home to make ends meet, it was with the help of good neighbors and her mother that eliminated worries about how the baby was cared for while she worked. Fully aware of how selfish Blanch was, Lydia made the conscious choice to hide finances from her daughter and make it clear to Blanch that if she chose to go to college, the expense was hers alone. Lydia had had enough of her oldest child's antics.

By the time Kimberlee started school, her sister had moved on to her new life. Blanch would never visit the home she shared with Lydia and Kimberlee. She would avoid any chance of ever seeing her child again.

Lydia raised Kimberlee with love and compassion as her guide while her daughter moved along her path. Kimberlee would be one of many casualties Blanch's self-absorption would leave in her wake and would eventually be her undoing.

Blanch

CHAPTER 2

Since the time of her birth, Blanch always had the desire to control everything. She had refused to breastfeed, preferring only bottled formula. Should the temperature of her meal not suit her palate, endless crying ensued. Her parents, Lydia and Frank, knew within a very short amount of time, their lives would be full of challenges with this child. With the constant crying from Blanch and Lydia's complaints about his not working, Frank exited the women's lives when Blanch reached three months of age. He decided Blanch was too much trouble and opted out of the family lifestyle. His clothes packed, Frank walked out the front door leaving mother and child behind to fend for themselves.

In her late thirties, Lydia did her best to raise her daughter to be a decent member of society. Never managing to gain control of her willful offspring, Lydia found her child to be extremely tiresome. As she grew, only one time did Blanch question where her father was. Lydia's explanation to her child invoked a disdainful retort. "I never needed him anyway," the five-year-old child stated pragmatically. That would be the last time Blanch would ever speak of her father.

Blanch never developed an affection for men; in her opinion, they only served one purpose, sexual satisfaction. Becoming sexually active at the age of thirteen, by her own choice, she quickly discovered what her body desired. No discussion was had with her mother about sexual practices or preventative measures regarding pregnancy; it was not necessary as Blanch thought she knew what was best. The lack of communication on the topic left Lydia unaware her daughter was menstruating at thirteen years old. This secret was just one of the many ways Blanch maintained complete control of her life. She was incredibly private about how she managed her body. In her way of thinking, it wasn't any of her mother's business what she chose to do.

At a very young age, Blanch was aware her looks didn't garner the attention of others as she hoped. She learned early on to utilize wit and manipulation to obtain what she wanted from others. Blanch always rejected Lydia's attempts to help her daughter improve her looks. Even with her mother working extra hours to pay for the dental work Blanch severely needed, she didn't want the intervention of outsiders. So self-focused on doing things her own way, three months into the process of straightening her teeth, Blanch stood in front of a cracked mirror in her garage, removing each brace with a pair of pliers. She decided she would not wear them; the fact her teeth resembled a poorly seeded row of corn was not enough to convince her she needed them. With the exception of her misaligned teeth, she was not unattractive but indeed not a cover model. Her skin was the color of a light pink rose and free from blemishes. When she enhanced her outline with the right clothing, her well-proportioned body allowed her to be noticed. Opting to wear a single color of eye shadow alongside very pale lipstick forced focus to her curves. She believed her figure provided her with great power over the opposite sex. Her teenage friends, most of whom looked like a Picasso painting, wore as many colors on their faces as possible. Blanch understood the impact of looking unique; she desired to stand out in a crowd, and she sought to be different. It gave her a hidden strength and caused people to always remember who she was.

The tops she chose to wear were fitted to her waist to enhance her ample breast. She made a conscious effort for the pair to be noticed when necessary. Her blonde hair, most often pulled into a chignon or braid, forced the unwitting onlooker to focus on her chest. The buttons on her blouse were often adjusted throughout the day; the number unbuttoned was dependent on whether her teacher was male or female. Blanch's innate ability to circumvent obstacles in her path often determined how much cleavage she revealed. She was not opposed to letting a male superior think he had the upper hand when in reality, she was always the one in control of the situation. A tight skirt, high heels, and partially exposed boobs allowed her supremacy when dealing with the male ego. Blanch preyed on men's sexual appetites; her skillset honed daily to support her desire to do as she pleased.

Even though she was not considered a classic beauty by other women, the allure she carried appealed to men. A part of this attraction was her bold and outspoken behavior around them; this strong will would serve her well in the future. The other trick she often utilized was the subtle way she touched a man when speaking to him, never anything overt, in public. Blanch believed she could tap into their carnal urges, eventually leading them to perform any task she desired.

Lydia was appalled at how her daughter flaunted herself at men. Sensing nothing good would come from this behavior; she tried repeatedly to convince her child to avoid such attention. Just as with the warning to not covet the neighbor's ass, Blanch had no concerns about what her mother's warnings were. This was her way out from under her mother's roof; the goal was to find a man with the means to take her far away.

Spring break freshman year of high school was in full swing. Blanch was having fun at the

Meadowbrook Country Club swimming pool, flashing her skimpy bikini to its patrons. She managed access to the club by carefully selecting and befriending a girl she attended school with. With ten weeks of classes remaining when they returned, Blanch was making the most of her time away from her studies. She spent as much time as possible away from home, hanging out with her friend, Tessa.

Tessa and her family arrived in Palestine shortly after Tessa was born. Her dad relocated the family to the small town when the need to take over his father's law firm arose. It wasn't until high school the girls first met, as Blanch was from the other side of the tracks. Once Blanch was aware that Tessa's father was wealthy and good-looking, she did anything she could to befriend the girl.

When Blanched noticed Tessa's father ogling the young girls during a fall basketball game, the intensity of their friendship swelled. From that moment forward, Blanch made it a point to always hug Tessa's father tightly anytime salutations were in play. She subtly rubbed her breasts to and fro against him until she felt his pants begin to swell from being aroused. It was never her intent to have sex with him; the flirtation was merely one of her many manipulations. Noticing the erection in her father's trousers after one of Blanch's hugs, Tessa confronted Blanch regarding her behavior around her dad. Blanch, in a naive fashion, said she was unaware the man liked her that way. By the end of Blanch's soliloquy, Tessa was in tears thinking it was her father who was the bad seed.

On day two of lounging by the pool with Tessa at the country club, Blanch spotted the man she would pursue, attempting to fulfill her desire to leave her mother's home. Seeing him walk past the pool wearing a white linen shirt and tightly fitted khaki linen pants, she initially assumed he to be staff. His pants fit him in such a way Blanch found herself fantasizing about the fun they would have in a bungalow on the property. On her initial sighting, she sensed he would merely be a good fuck.

Following him with her eyes across the landscape, pure lust in her heart, her interest shifted when he sat across from her friend's father at the bar. Her assumption of his position had been incorrect. Blanch had eyes on her prey.

Entering the lounge area where the two men sat, Blanch allowed her swimsuit cover to gape open, revealing her cleavage. Approaching Tessa's father, she claimed Tessa sent her to find out when they would leave the club that afternoon. Making it clear to the stranger she was not related to his table mate at the bar, she slunk away back to the pool after retrieving an answer. Gabriel's attraction to the young girl was quickly noted by the man he sat next to.

"She has one hell of a body, doesn't she?" He spoke slowly while assessing the tightened muscles on Gabriel's face.

"She is muy, how do you say, attractive. ¿No?" Gabriel's smile grew broad while continuing to watch Blanch return to the poolside lounge chair. She let her cover-up slide down her arms, landing on the padded chaise lounge. Her pink swimsuit faintly revealed the large dark brown aureolas through its thin material.

"She always rubs up against my cock when she greets me; I can't wait for the opportunity to fuck her." The smirk on his colleague's face was offensive to Gabriel as he felt she was his prize. The line in the sand had been drawn; the unspoken competition between the two men for who would bed her first had begun. Gabriel had never lost when it came to capturing a woman's favor.

Gabriel Laverde was easily fifteen years Blanch's senior. He came from old money, was well-educated, and incredibly charming. His visit to the country club to meet Tessa's father was for business. His company's interest in establishing a small factory in Texas for tax purposes needed the lawyer's expertise. This venture bringing him to the States from Columbia, was to strike a deal with the city for a tax break. Tessa's father was on retention to manage the contracts for the new site.

Most of his life had been spent on the border of Columbia and Panama; his earthy good looks intrigued Blanch. His skin tone was dark and perfectly smooth. Gabriel's lineage was a combination of his father from Spain and his mother from an island in the Caribbean. His square jaw was in perfect proportion to his dimpled chin and thin lips. He reminded her of a statue of David carved out of onyx. She was drawn to his brown eyes, dark wavy hair, and perfectly aligned white teeth. At five feet eleven inches tall, he towered over her. His frame was unique to Blanch; she had never witnessed a man who was not thick in the middle. With the exception of Tessa's father, all the men she had encountered in Texas had no differentiation between the width of hips and waistline; this man's waist was smaller than his hips, elongating his torso to his groin.

This was the first time a man had ever consumed her full attention. Blanch concluded if she was going to trap a man into marrying her, she might as well catch the perfect male specimen. Blanch's looks and speech portrayed her as a woman in her early twenties; Gabriel never thought to ask.

Initially, he thought he should be coy and spend time seducing her slowly. Then it occurred to him that the chance to see her again was unknown. With that realization, a twenty-dollar tip given to a waiter at the club ensured a note was delivered to the young woman. The message contained the name of his hotel alongside a key to his room. This simple invitation was all that was needed to make certain they would meet again. By the time Gabriel finished his afternoon meeting, and his third martini, Blanch was naked in his hotel bed, legs spread, waiting for him.

Entering the room, he was pleasantly surprised to find her in his bed, masturbating, moaning out loud. Seeing him stand in the bedroom doorway of the suite, observing her ritual, she begged him to penetrate her. Gabriel didn't bother to take his pants off; he merely unzipped the linen trousers and took her from the edge of the bed. As Gabriel began to ejaculate, he pulled out of Blanch. Leaving his semen on the floor next to the bed, she was disappointed. This was not part of her plan. She was, however, grateful for his stamina as she took him three more times that night before going home. She mounted him each time to ensure he would deliver his sperm inside her. She told him she had no concerns over getting pregnant; he assumed she was referring to birth control. As she dressed to leave, she kissed him on the cheek and then stroked his ego. "I have never had a man as big as you. It was like the first time! Was it good for you, too?"

Lying to her mother that she was staying with Tessa, she returned to the hotel every night for the rest of her spring break, providing pleasure for the both of them. Upon entering the hotel each evening, she made sure the desk clerk knew which room she was going to and who she was going to see. When she left Gabriel after their love-making sessions, she would stop back by the desk to make sure the clerk saw her in a disheveled state. She hoped the man behind the desk would call the police and report this young girl who was obviously participating in sexual activities within the hotel. This manipulation failed as the man behind the desk assumed she was a prostitute, hopeful he would get a turn with her after Gabriel checked out.

Spring break over, everyone returned to school with stories to share about their adventures during the time off. Blanch's version of her vacation was uneventful; she claimed nothing exciting happened. Returning to school did not reduce the amount of time spent with her prospective future husband while he was in town. Determined to keep her mother in the dark for as long as possible, Blanch used school activities as the reason she was late arriving home every day.

Negotiations with the city wrapped up sooner than Blanch expected; it was time for Gabriel to return to his home in South America. With the tax abatements agreed to, the new facility could be built the following year.

Gabriel was quite satisfied with his new playmate and had hopes of future sexual encounters during his visits to Texas. Four weeks later, when he returned, Blanch put her plan into action. His visit to start his project would unexpectedly be cut short.

CHAPTER 3

Missing her second period in a row, Blanch was convinced she was pregnant. Sitting her mother down, she confessed to being sexually active. Sharing the news with her mother was just part of her plan. Now that Lydia knew, Blanch assumed her mother would have no choice but to force the father to marry her young daughter. Lydia's reaction was completely opposite of what Blanch had hoped. She directed Blanch to pack her bags immediately; Blanch would live with her grandmother, far away from town, until the baby was born.

With her plans unexpectedly altered, Blanch quickly had to reconfigure her strategy. She would go to the hotel, tell Gabriel the news and force his hand. What else could he do? A foreigner from South America visiting this country had taken advantage of an impressionable young girl. His business relations would be ruined should he not marry her and save her reputation.

That was her story, and she had well rehearsed its performance.

Sneaking out her bedroom window at home, she made her way to the hotel. She determined a knock on the suite door was all it would take to resolve the challenge. Avoiding the man at the front desk on this visit, she was now standing in the hallway outside Gabriel's room. Raising her hand to rap on the hotel room door, she heard Gabriel's voice in the hallway coming towards his room. She then heard a woman's laughter accompanying his remarks. Turning to look where the sound was coming from, she was stunned to see Tessa's mother arm in arm with Gabriel. She quietly retreated before they noticed her at the entrance to his room.

Blanch needed to realign her plan again.

Quickly devising an alternate scheme, she quietly departed the hotel through a side door, making her way to Tessa's home. Her thought was that with Tessa's father serving as Gabriel's counsel, he would be forced to take Blanch and confront Gabriel. Explaining her situation to the man,

Tessa's dad became outraged to hear young Blanch had been defiled; his rage was driven by the fact he had not been the one to have her first. Blinded by anger, he pulled Blanch from the home's front porch to the car in the driveway. In the car, they were quickly on their way to the hotel to confront Gabriel in person. Blanch never mentioned to Tessa's father that Gabriel had company.

"He will own up to what he has done and make this right!" Speaking with righteous indignation, he kept calling her poor Blanch, a child taken advantage of. Arriving at the hotel, Blanch was dragged past the lobby clerk she had engaged with so many times. Reaching Gabriel's room, Blanch held tightly by the arm, Tessa's father knocked on the door. As the door began to open, his grip on poor Blanch loosened. His wife was holding the doorknob from the other side, dressed only in her bra and panties. Taking a long drag on her cigarette, she began to tremble, seeing someone other than room service at the door.

Observing the reaction of the married couple to each other, Blanch produced an impish grin. Proud of herself for the execution of her latest scheme.

Gabriel exited the bathroom baring his naked body to his unknown guest. His playmate retreated from her husband, her nose bloody, her eyes swelling as she recoiled from his assault. The next punch, rapidly approaching his wife's face, slowed upon seeing Gabriel in the bathroom doorway. Momentarily stunned to see his business liaison, the man whom his wife was fucking was now known. Blind rage overtook him; he began pummeling his wife with sheer madness. Gabriel quickly grabbed the crazed husband from behind; forgetting he was naked, he pulled the man towards the hallway. Gabriel, now in the corridor exposing his near-perfect body to all who had stepped from their rooms to witness the commotion, pinned the madman to the floor.

Blanch casually made her way through the hotel suite to the bedroom, allowing the chaos to be her cover. She quietly collected the woman's clothes and headed for the huddled mass lying on the floor of the living area. Handing Tessa's mother her outfit, Blanch suggested the soon-to-be divorcee dress before the police arrived. In shock from being struck by her husband, the mistress never realized the young girl helping her was Tessa's friend. Looking up from the bloodied woman on the floor, Blanch looked to the door to see the lobby clerk observing the room. She quickly disappeared into the bedroom closet, where she would remain until it was safe to reveal herself.

After the police finished their questioning and the room was once again calm, Gabriel poured himself a cocktail. Now in his boxer shorts, he sat down on one of the sofas in the living area to determine his next move. He couldn't stay in Texas any longer than necessary. By the time dinner had been served in the homes of Palestine, Texas, every husband in town would know about his sexual prowess. Tessa's mother was not the only white woman in Texas he bedded on his visits.

Gabriel decided it was best he return to his home in Cali. He would send a replacement to finish up the deal he had initiated. Contracts had been executed; the rest of the work could be handled by his brother-in-law. The gringo his sister had married was a part of the family business; he felt confident the white man would be able to resolve the issue and salvage their plans for the US factory.

Realizing he would have to be more thoughtful about his sexual conquest in the future, he determined he was lucky not to have been killed. Gabriel wasn't married and had no desire to be, so sleeping with multiple partners was not an issue for him. He liked being single and enjoyed the company of women whenever he chose. He worked, played, and had no desire to be a father.

An epiphany of a simple truth occurred to him; Gabriel would have to learn the meaning of discretion. After a few phone calls were made, the flight out of Dallas was booked for the following day. He would leave early in the morning before anyone realized he had gone. No charges had been filed against him by the police; leaving sooner than later was just a precaution in case any other men found out what their wives had been doing.

Pouring himself a refresher, he pondered what would happen to the woman he had just serviced. Taking a drink, he moved from the living room towards the bedroom doors. He didn't recall them being closed but couldn't confirm their position one way or the other. Sliding a door open, he was surprised to find Blanch in his bed. The drink in his hand was not strong enough to numb him from the reminder of another poor choice.

"I am in no mood for company. You need to go." Gabriel was polite but firm.

"Oh, I'm not going anywhere, and I am pretty sure you aren't either." Blanch was smugly delivering her mandate. "I am fourteen years old and am carrying your child. Surely you want to take care of your unborn child and me." Blanch forced her lips into a pouting position merely for effect. "Where are we going to call home?"

Gabriel had been in these situations before; this time, the girl claimed to be a minor. Never revealing the concern running through his mind, he smiled at her. An Afro-Latino impregnating a white girl in rural Texas would most likely end with him swinging from a noose dangling from the end of a tree branch. He doubted this situation was one the police would understand so easily. Never mind that she had seduced him; it was his stupidity for not asking her age.

"Do you want to have a baby at your young age? There are options?" Gabriel was hoping a cool and calm approach would sway Blanch to be reasonable.

"Of course, I want to have your baby. I will love being your wife and raising our child!" Blanch continued to pout at him while she spoke.

Gabriel excused himself from the bedroom under the guise, he wanted another drink. Moving to the living area, he pondered how he should handle this. He recognized Blanch was manipulating him. Damn, his easily aroused libido!

After making another cocktail, he returned to the bedroom to find her sprawled on the bed, manipulating her genitals. His libido didn't stir this time as he was now fully aware of her ability to mold events to suit her wants. He reclined on the chair across from the bed and observed her while sipping his drink. Putting all the pieces of the afternoon together, he was now fully aware of her ability to create chaos. She was the one who brought Tessa's father to the hotel. She was a strong-willed young girl who would stop at nothing to get what she wanted.

Confused by his lack of participation on top of the sheets, Blanch began to whimper at him. Gabriel continued with his libation without speaking a word. His experience with a strong-willed woman had taught him a thing or two. He had to decide whether to let her think she had him under her control or force her into a rage. He just needed enough time to meet his plane and return to Columbia. A third option he had not considered appeared with a knock on the room's front door.

He rose from the chair while requesting Blanch continue servicing herself. "I will join you when I have answered the door and finished my drink." His promise whispered in her ear allowed Blanch to relax and focus on the pleasure she was creating with her fingertips. Exiting the room, he slid the pocket doors closed before making his way across the room.

The woman standing in the hallway was unexpected. Matronly in appearance, she was older than he by at least 20 years. Her simple a-line dress did not hide her curvy plumpness. For a moment, he thought she was a maid. He began to dismiss her; no one could know Blanch was in his bed or what she was doing.

"Good evening, I am Blanch's mother. Her friend Tessa called me and said her father had left her at the hotel. If I know my daughter, she is still here."

Gabriel graciously invited Lydia into the room. The invitation confirmed Blanch's presence in the hotel. He wasn't quite sure of the intentions of the young girl's mother but sensed he had no choice but to listen to her.

"My daughter has been trouble from the day she was conceived. I have tried everything I could to control her and get her on the right path. I suspect you are the father of her baby, and my question is, do you want anything to do with it or her?"

By now, Blanch had stopped masturbating; she recognized the voice in the other room. She was trapped; her mother could spoil the entire plan. Rising from the bed, she made her way to the door. She wanted to hear every word muttered between the two adults. Reaching to slide the door ajar to listen in on their conversation, she was startled when it quickly slid open, her mother on the opposite side.

"This man doesn't want you or the child. Get your clothes on; we are leaving. If you cause a scene or create any more trouble for this man, I will have you committed to a psychiatric institution as a nymphomaniac. Between Tessa's father and this man, I am sure that can be easily arranged."

Blanch quietly left the hotel and was soon on her way to live with her grandmother. She didn't have a choice, and her manipulations had failed. She was in shock that her plan did not come together. For the first time in her life, she was lost and without hope.

Lydia returned to Palestine without her child three days later. Making her way to the high school's principal's office to explain Blanch's absence, she wondered what the future looked like for her daughter.

Lydia explained why Blanch would be out for the remainder of the school year; her grandmother needed Blanch to help with the farm. "My father has recently passed, and I need Blanch there to help out emotionally and physically." Asking the school to allow Blanch to do her work from there was uncommon, but it was only six more weeks until summer break, and she felt sure the principal would be happy not to have to deal with her child.

The principal agreed to work something out for the rest of the year. His eager agreement was driven by his being a victim of Blanch's attention as well; he saw this as his way out of a potentially bad situation. With his pending move to a new school in Virginia, he would benefit from Blanch being out of pocket until the school year was complete.

Living with her grandmother, sulking over her plan that fell apart, she spent most moments awake going over her actions. She needed to understand where she had failed. What critical steps had she missed? She vowed never to fail to achieve what she wanted again.

Lydia visited the farm on weekends and was not surprised when Blanch emphatically told her she did not want the child growing inside her. "Give the bastard away or let me get an abortion!" she repeatedly stated. Lydia finally came to an agreement with her daughter; Lydia would raise the child leaving Blanch free to focus on school. Lydia made no pretenses with Blanch; she had had enough. With the conditions in place, Blanch would never speak of having a baby and would limit her engagement with the child. Once she finished high school, she could do whatever she wanted as long as she left home and promised never to return.

"This child deserves a life without your nonsense. I have allowed you to get away with too much. All because I felt guilty that your daddy left us. You will take no more of my heart from me!" Lydia cried as she spoke the harsh words, but she knew it had to be said for the unborn child's sake.

Blanch was thrilled to hear her mother's verbal separation from her. She didn't want her mother involved in her life going forward anyway.

CHAPTER 4

Shortly after Kimberlee was born, the solution to Blanch's quandary presented itself to her. The path out of this small-town life she despised so deeply was to attend college far away where no one knew her or her family. At the beginning of her sophomore year of high school, Blanch sought out the help of a female high school counselor. She wanted honest answers without a male ego getting in the mix. The counselor was brutally direct with her; junior college was the only option unless Blanch improved her GPA to a minimum of a 3.0. At best, she had managed C's and D's in her studies; she never realized the importance of school and its impact on the rest of her life. She had the ability; her counselor was well aware of how incredibly smart Blanch was and quickly pointed out she had never applied the energy required for success. Blanch never thought there was a need; now she understood there was. Blanch's pinpoint focus on leaving this town she loathed left no room for encumbrances.

Returning to school after summer break, Blanch was surprised Tessa wouldn't speak to her. Tessa did her research and was reasonably sure Blanch was the root cause of why she lost her family unit. She didn't have all the facts, but her hindsight being 20/20 and the tiny bits of information her parents shared, she was reasonably sure Blanch knew her mom was sleeping with the South-American man.

Blanch had not considered the impact on her social life by losing her friend; she also didn't realize the scorn headed her way. Tessa not only took away the country club life but also the other friendships she had delivered to Blanch. Blanch was forced into being a loner. Tessa was far more intelligent than Blanch had given her credit for; she would be a worthy adversary in this game called life. Entirely alone now, her resolve to get away from the small town strengthened.

Kimberlee adored Blanch. Whenever Blanch arrived home, the baby would crawl towards her, craving Blanch's attention. After a quick pass through the kitchen to grab a snack,

Blanch would walk straight to her room and close the door, never acknowledging the young child's desire for attention. From the moment Kimberlee exited Blanch's body, the child was rejected by her now "sister."

Growing quickly into a fast-moving toddler who kept her mother busy, it was exhausting for Lydia to work and raise the small child. Blanch's emotional and physical distance from her mother created additional stress for Lydia. Blanch did not help at home, leaving the task of running a house with a small child on her mother's shoulders.

Seeing the challenges laid upon her daughter, Lydia's mother closed up the farmhouse and moved into the city with her daughter. This was a great relief to both of the women; the companionship and sharing of the daily responsibilities made life bearable for each of them.

Lydia's father had been a wise businessman, looking to the future for his wife and child; the remaining five hundred acres of East Texas land he held on to had been leased to tenant farmers. The contractual commitment from the farmers ensured his wife would need for nothing after his death. The money made from the land covered basic expenses for the widow, put a little aside for investing while allowing her the luxury to live with and support her daughter. An unexpected outcome of his working hard and not splurging on luxuries was that Blanch assumed the family was poor and lacked funds to acquire anything beyond the basic necessities of life. Lydia left Blanch to believe the assumption; she would not allow Blanch access to the hard-earned money her parents had amassed. She was confident her daughter would quickly squander it away.

Blanch knew whatever path she chose beyond high school would be her choice, and she would bear the cost associated with it; her mother had made that quite clear before Kimberlee was born. Keeping the funds a mystery supported Lydia's desire for Blanch to make her own way and hopefully learn that there is a cost with every choice.

Just before Kimberlee's third birthday, Blanch graduated high school. She did not achieve Valedictorian status in her class of 186 students as she had hoped but did manage to graduate in the top five academically. Her position at number three was an amazing achievement, considering the antics of her freshman year. Her last-minute induction to the National Honor Society was her only other accolade on graduation day. Having become a recluse during her last three years of school, few people acknowledged she still attended their school. At her request, her mother and Kimberlee did not attend her graduation. Blanch felt she had done this all on her own and wanted to keep it that way. Pushing her family away was hurtful to everyone involved in her life. The two older women in her home hoped Blanch would mature and come to understand the importance of family and that hard lessons learned were necessary; for Blanch, the family was merely a means to an end and nothing more. Within days of graduation, Blanch was packed and on her way to university.

Accepted to the University of North Texas in Denton, just north of Dallas, she was finally on her way out of the little town she despised. Without input or influence from her family, Blanch chose to attend UNT over the three other colleges granting her admission. Through a collection of scholarship applications and Pell grants, she managed enough money to pay for her first year. Leaving her family behind was without emotion for her. A polite hug for her mom at the bus station was all she could manage. Blanch had come to realize she didn't hate her mother; she just didn't have any further use for her. Kimberlee cried tears she couldn't possibly understand while watching her big sister get on the bus without a goodbye.

Kimberlee and her mom would go on to live their lives without Blanch in it. The final time Lydia reached out to Blanch was to inform her that her grandmother had passed away. Blanch thanked her mom for the information and hung up the phone.

Blanch did well in her first year of college. She maintained a 3.2 GPA, which was amazing for a freshman from a small-town school system. She didn't socialize with any girls and avoided all sorority activities. She instead found comfort in hanging out with the boys. By accident, she had signed up for an elective in woodworking. A misplaced number on an enrollment sheet would take her places she never imagined.

At first, she wanted to drop the class but found herself intrigued by the machines and how they operated. She decided to stick it out, which led her to make several male friends. She also discovered she had a knack for communicating with men. It was all straightforward, with nothing subversive going on; they said what they meant and didn't care if they offended. Blanch appreciated this brash approach to communication. She had begun to mature and realized the games played in high school were foolish and naive.

She did not focus her energy on boyfriends leaving most people to assume she was a lesbian. When asked about her sexual orientation, her reply was always delivered over a giggle, "I like dick way too much!"

She sought out a couple of older boys who would provide for her sexual needs. The age difference was just enough to ensure it was never anything beyond sex. Perfect for the boys as well as for her; no commitments ever made by anyone. During the birth of her child in that East Texas farmhouse without medical attention, something happened to her female organs. With the use of the pill and her body's alteration, she would remain childless. She didn't know why and didn't question it. She was content believing she would never produce offspring again.

Excelling in her wood shop class, her professor encouraged her mechanical inclination and suggested she check into the engineering program. Blanch thanked him for the suggestion but was adamant about getting a business degree in finance. She was good with numbers and wanted a career in a leadership role; her goal of earning an MBA was the path she was on. She was somewhat intrigued by his suggestion which led her to use

elective credits in various mechanic-based courses. Unknowingly, this would be the portal to her
future.

A biology classmate who had a severe crush
on her made an attempt to get in good with her.
Mentioning an opening in the finance department
at his father's factory led to an hour spent with
Blanch sucking him off in her dorm room. After
his organ returned to its flaccid state, Blanch
kissed him sweetly on the lips and requested he
set up an interview for her at the company.

Bob Fergus was impressed with the young
girl from the moment he met her. He believed
Blanch had the necessary skill sets to assist his
wife, Joanne, in the accounting department.
Blanch received the job offer on the spot.

Joanne was happy to see her husband hire
a woman to work in the accounting department.
She learned of Blanch's goal to receive a finance
degree and work towards an MBA; she was excited to have a bright, young, somewhat plain girl
helping her with the bookkeeping.

Blanch quickly learned the financial aspects of the business from Joanne before moving on to learn the other parts of the business from top to bottom. From the manufacturing processes and their functions to sales and distribution. It was all very easy for her, and she was content for the first time in her life. Fergus Manufacturing quickly became her family.

With graduation from UNT in her sights, the owner did not want to lose his prize employee. Bob Fergus offered to pay for her MBA if she would commit five more years to him. His motivation was simple; he would continue to enjoy her sexual expertise while subtly offering a touch of hush money; he didn't want his children to discover his intimate explorations with Blanch while on business trips.

With the title of General Manager for the small manufacturing company on her nameplate, work required a lot more from her. She remained focused on school, work, and the occasional playmate. Beyond the time spent in her classes, she spent most waking moments helping with sales calls or participating in manufacturing. These two essential pieces of the business often had issues that required solving; Blanch adored the challenges. The camaraderie skills acquired while hanging out with the boys in college served her well. She knew how to appropriately cut up with the boys in the boardroom while gently tickling their balls under the conference table; this allowed her to get her way most of the time. She balanced relationships perfectly; Blanch did not sleep with the clients but left them thinking it might happen if they did as she asked.

A deep-seated fear of being perceived as inadequate drove her spirit. Recalling how she failed miserably with the trap she set in high school pushed her to learn everything she could about manufacturing. Not only how the business functioned but all the pieces of the puzzle required to run a successful company. She became so well-versed she could debate any aspect of manufacturing personal-care products. Her vast knowledge also allowed her the ability to sniff out anyone trying to bullshit her. Those who would dare attempt to manipulate her were her favorite people to take to task. The thrill of humiliating them and taking control of the situation was more pleasurable to her than any sexual encounter she had ever had, including Gabriel.

Blanch became extremely valuable to her boss; he not only admired her performance skills in the bedroom but saw her as capable of running his company in the future.

Often times the mutterings of employees would make their way to the conference room. A particular rumor was repeatedly noted; employees suspected the future president of Fergus of being the owner's illegitimate daughter. She never spoke of a family on any level; her past was a mystery. Blanch never addressed the notion they were related; this rumor provided cover for the real reason they often traveled together and the abundant time spent behind closed doors.

The rumor mill was often fed information via Blanch's assistant, Bobby. Often times Blanch would direct him to deliver certain bits of information. Bobby liked being held in confidence by the elitist leadership team; he was perceived to be clueless to the fact he was being used for his boss's gain.

Bobby was a fun-loving, outgoing, thick around the, waist, middle-aged queen who was incredibly charming. For a large man, Bobby presented himself very well. Always dressed in the latest couture, he was quite proficient in charming the pants off of any man he wanted. If Blanch ever suspected a man swung both ways, she would put Bobby on his tail. (You should pardon the expression.) Her pile of dirt for future dealings with these men always needed replenishing. Bobby was adept at gathering information while partaking in post-coitus conversation; he considered himself a part of the grand scheme Blanch was developing.

Over cocktails one evening, Blanch foolishly shared a conversation with him about her long-term plans. She thought herself to be coy enough that Bobby would assume she to be daydreaming. Blanch mistook him for being dense; she assumed he was unable to connect the dots of her ultimate goal. Bobby played dumb very well, but he was anything but foolish. He suspected he was being used for her personal gain; he didn't mind as long as there was a reward in it for him as well. He would play his role as required.

Two years passed while Bobby collated the necessary list of men with money who would help them achieve her dream. Getting financial support from these individuals was critical; some would engage voluntarily, others by coercion. All who participated had fallen victim to Blanch's successful manipulation tactics.

CHAPTER 5

Employees, alongside their customers, became overly concerned for their future when Bob Fergus passed unexpectedly. No one expected a man of sixty-two years old to die from a stroke. He had been a lively man who worked long hours and fully participated in life. Greatly appreciated by all who knew him, regardless of wealth or social status, he treated everyone as an equal. His flaws in life were typical of his gender; cigars on occasion, a cocktail or glass of wine every evening, and a companion other than his wife. He and his wife had long ago agreed to stay married for the sake of their children but allowed each other to live out their personal fantasies as long as it was kept quiet. Joanne had her lovers; Bob had his.

No one had ever thought to suggest Fergus create a disaster contingency plan for the organization. With his passing, customers were now at the mercy of new leadership.

Upon Bob Fergus' death, the company immediately put his oldest child in charge as CEO. Blanch's old friend from college was now her boss. Andrew had no interest in running the organization; he enjoyed what he was doing within the business.

Joining the sales team after graduation with his Bachelor's Degree in Business, he wanted nothing more. He liked the playful nature of the sales job and the paycheck that went with it. The salesman's salary was secondary to supporting his wants and needs; it was the money he received monthly from the family coffers that supported his lavish lifestyle. His sales numbers never justified his $110,000 annual salary; his position and pay were pure and simple nepotism. Now in the position of leadership, he found himself lacking the know-how to run the company and keep it afloat. He turned to Blanch, just as she had hoped he would.

Bob Fergus' verbal promise, along with a well-performed act of fellatio on his son, provided Blanch the title of President of the company. As

CEO, Andrew offered her a significant pay increase along with equity in the company; Blanch declined the offer to take the large salary; it was the equity she was after. "The company would be better suited to increase the equity portion of the offer. If I am not successful as President, then no money is lost. If I am able to meet the goals we set out, then I will receive my earnings at the end of each year from the profits."

The former salesman now turned CEO, discussed the matter, after the fact, with his mother and sister. Joanne's managing of the books through the years, as the company grew, allowed her to take a backseat in the organization after Blanch joined the team. Even though removed from the day-to-day, she felt Blanch's assessment was a strong argument for success. They needed to keep the cash flow strong; the family needed its monthly paycheck to maintain the lives they so enjoyed. After chastising her son for making the offer prior to consulting with the family, she agreed to Andrew's plan.

Blanch was promoted to President. The legal documents executed gave her 25% equity in the company. The remaining 75% of the company belonged to the widow and her two children; 35%, 20%, and 20%, respectively.

Blanch quickly settled into the leadership role she had sought after so long. She began her campaign to expand the capabilities of the business offerings, looking to set the company up for long-term growth. Directing the sales team to seek out unique processes other companies deemed unprofitable was the starting point of her master plan.

Fergus Manufacturing soon gained a reputation as an entity that would take on problem products. Her ploy worked, and Fergus Manufacturing began being noticed by industry leaders. Press releases touted the ability to solve any challenge presented, "Fergus will find a solution!" was their anthem. With this new focus on growth, the sales and project management teams grew at a rapid pace. Blanch personally attended equipment auctions with the company's mechanical

team. Only after her approval would they purchase the previously owned machines, quickly
expanding operations and capacity by fifty percent within her first year as President. As the
used machines continued to arrive on their docks,
the search for additional space began. An additional fifty-thousand square feet was necessary in
order for manufacturing to function. The facility
had quickly been filled from wall to wall with
equipment and was no longer safe nor functional.
All the expansion of resources, both human and
mechanical, led to money flowing out faster than
it could be earned.

As a privately held company, the owners
had willingly accepted Blanch's five-year plan.
She had been clear the first three years operating
at a loss was part of the investment phase.
Joanne was the first to see the brilliance in
Blanch's long-term plan. She did not, however,
expect the expenses for equipment to consume as
much cash as they did.

Cash flow quickly became a significant issue
for the company; hard decisions had to be made

promptly. Family members would either reduce their monthly financial drain on the company or use their personal assets as collateral for a business loan. Neither of Bob Fergus' children wanted to reduce the income they received monthly; they voted to forward Blanch's business plan and override their mother's wishes to pull back.

As a mother and majority stake holder, Joanne made the difficult choice to provide her kids with what they wanted. A major piece of Joanne's personal property became collateral in the amount of $10,000,000. Joanne Fergus' personal home, the estate her family left her, was now tied to Fergus Manufacturing; the expansive residence's deed was now held by a bank.

With an open-ended expense account and little consideration for the risk his mother had taken, the CEO rarely showed up at the office any longer. He trusted his college friend to take care of things and ensure the company succeeded. In his mind, Blanch had skin in the game and wouldn't benefit from the company failing. Blindly approving any request Blanch made, he inadvertently handed control of the company over to her.

Joanne Fergus' long-time concern over the spending and lack of return into the business grew after a quarterly tax review came into her possession. An unscheduled visit to see Blanch was in order.

Making her way through the offices, Mrs. Fergus passed the cubicles leading toward the executive suites. Stopping at the Controller's office, she demanded access to inspect the books. After all, she was the original CFO of Fergus Manufacturing. It didn't take her long to realize she had made a mistake by not staying involved in the day-to-day of the business. Without her knowledge, Blanch had altered the accounting software and ledger system Joanne had implemented. The system utilized was now a series of complicated T-accounts that were difficult to follow. With her home in Dallas used as collateral, she feared for her future and her children's. With the family maintaining controlling interest in the company, she relaxed somewhat. Ultimately believing they had time to resolve the issue before the company went bankrupt.

Blanch knew this day was coming; she hoped it wouldn't happen for another year or more. She still needed time to implement her scheme fully. Entering the Controller's office with a smile and willingness to answer any question that arose, Blanch greeted Joanne with a hug. "Joanne, I have been as transparent as I can with you. The financial plan I laid out for the expansion is on track. The family knew there was a minimum of three years before we would see a payback." Blanch gently touched Joanne on the hand while offering up a sympathetic smile.

"I understand your concern about the remaining eight million dollars leveraged against your home." She worked hard to conceal her emotions while speaking to Joanne.

Mrs. Fergus couldn't read Blanch. She wasn't sure if there was real concern by the young woman she had trained or if it was just a show. Surely this sweet young woman would do the right thing. After all, when she walked in on

Blanch giving her husband a blowjob in his office, she made it clear it was of no concern to her. She even offered some advice to ensure he achieved ejaculation. She could have fired Blanch right then and there, and now she began questioning if she should have.

Blanch clung to Joanne tightly while escorting her to the front entrance of the building. This outward emotion triggered Joanne; Blanch had never been affectionate with her before. Leaving the facility with a polite goodbye, she pondered how to address the situation.

Parking her car in the drive of her heavily mortgaged home, she decided it was necessary to address her concerns with the co-owners of the business, her children. Paging them with the 911 code indicating they should each call immediately, she poured a glass of wine and settled into the desk chair in her home office to wait by the phone. Thirty minutes later, son and daughter were en route to the home they grew up in for a family discussion. Joanne laid out her concerns to the two kids, both of whom quietly listened while she shared her discoveries that day. Neither appeared as concerned as their mother.

The family meeting morphed into afternoon drinks before dinner at Avanti's. Hashing out business scenarios over Italian food with expensive red wine, Joanne's children did not appear to have any significant issue with Blanch's plans. As Joanne's Tiramisu arrived, her daughter smiled and said, "What's the issue, Mom? You don't really need that huge of a house anyway!"

Mrs. Fergus realized the conversation with her children was moot. They could not, or would not, understand the future implications of Blanch's actions. Joanne began to see the light; Blanch was incapable of doing the job, and she would have to force the young woman out. If she didn't take action, her replacement would likely sway the children to sell. With only 35% ownership in the company, the only real power she had, was to call in a favor at the bank in possession of the deed to her home. She would have to persuade the bank to call the note due. The kids would then be forced to join her in selling the company she and her husband had built. She no longer trusted Blanch; this would be the best way to get rid of her.

Before leaving for her home in Portugal on her annual pilgrimage, Joanne called a dear friend and invited her to lunch. Personal relationships in her world carried way more power than most realized; Joanne knew who would best be able to help her. She had been there for this woman when she had been sorely in need, and Joanne knew the woman could easily persuade her husband to assist in resolving the issue. Of course, this would mean a commitment to allow her friend to earn a commission from the sale of the business.

Sitting at a patio table at Parigi's, Joanne spotted her friend making her way past the Maître D'. Standing up, she kissed her friend on both cheeks as she arrived at the table. Settling back into her chair, she took a sip of the chilled white wine in front of her before she spoke. "My dear Tessa, thank you for seeing me on such short notice."

Tessa directed the waiter to pour her a glass of wine from the bottle resting on the table before responding. "Anything for you, my dear. I owe you so much for helping me when my mom died. What else is family for?"

Joanne told Tessa of the issue at the company and her plan to force it into being sold. Tessa was a prominent woman in the commercial real estate game in North Texas. Her connections and acumen allowed her insight into how this should unfold; the significantly large commission upon the sale of the company's property would be a feather in her cap. Her husband's litigation knowledge and his seat on the Board of Directors at the bank carrying the note made this all a no-brainer to Joanne.

When Joanne stopped going to the office every day and began to enjoy the fruits of her labors, she often bragged about the brilliant young woman allowing her freedom to do as she pleased; the name of the young woman taking her place had never come up in conversation with Tessa, until today.

When Joanne's cousin in East Texas was murdered by her husband, Joanne and Bob took the couple's only child into their care. Joanne went so far as to live with Tessa part-time so she could finish her senior year of high school. That year would have been unbearable for both of them had it not been for the kindness of a local woman who eagerly helped them.

Even with the news of Tessa's father on trial for murdering his wife following Tessa to Dallas, she proved herself a strong independent woman. Arriving at SMU, the silent whispers were constantly prevalent. She never forgot or forgave the woman who created the chaos that led to her mother being killed.

Hearing the name from her past, Tessa reached for her glass. Consuming the chilled liquid in one gulp, she took a deep breath before responding to her lunch partner. "I will be more than happy to help you with that little bitch." Joanne was surprised at the strong response from Tessa. She certainly appreciated the support given to her but quickly inquired why the aggressive tone. As Tessa shared the details of her past with Blanch, Joanne began to realize this might be more of a challenge than she had expected. She had confirmation that Blanch was devious and would be troublesome, and now she had the dirt to force her to go away quietly.

"Let's keep this under wraps until I am back from the Algarve. Talk to that sweet husband of yours about my scheme. I will want to move swiftly when I return."

The ladies sipped their wine, turning the conversation to society matters while having lunch. Discussing disturbing news of a friend in their inner circle who caught her husband in bed with the pool boy, each offered up prayers of pity for her. Joanne was thankful that her husband at least had the decency to sleep with other women.

The following day Joanne was seated in her private jet headed to Europe. Meanwhile, across town, Tessa explained what her dear cousin needed help with to her husband over breakfast.

It was but a few days later when Bobby was shocked to hear the loan was going to be forced on the company and even more intrigued about the juicy details surrounding his boss's behavior as a young girl. Oh, how he enjoyed his pillow talk with his long-time lover; now he had great dirt on his boss, something he had never achieved before. His wheels were spinning over how to use this information best as he kissed his partner goodbye. He was anxious to get home and get a good night's sleep for the next day's adventure.

Delivering her morning diet soda filled to the brim and ice swimming in it, Bobby sat across from his boss and shared the news of the impending takedown of the company. He saved the additional information he garnered from his fuck buddy for another day. He was sure there would be a reason he would need the details in the future.

Blanch absorbed the information, never verbalizing her displeasure to the news; her rage was obvious by observing her beet red décolletage and neck. She asked Bobby to excuse her and deny anyone's request to speak with or see her that day.

As code for the fact his boss was not in a happy place, Bobby had a little magnet he discreetly placed on the side of his desk where Blanch could not see it. A Halloween Witch on a broom indicated to anyone who neared the executive area to take heed and turn around.

For three days, Blanch laid low while setting out how to expedite the course of actions slotted for the following year. Everyone, including Bobby, was surprised when the current CEO and his sister arrived at the facility for a meeting with Blanch. He immediately knew he was no longer a part of the bigger picture.

Blanch spun the plan laid out by Joanne to her favor. She claimed that she completely understood why Joanne would want to protect her home and get out of the business. It was then that she explained to the two adult children of Bob Fergus that with the company in its current state of financial obligations, the call made for repayment would leave them bankrupt.

"I trust you two have planned well with your investments. If this proceeds, your assets are what you will be living off of. Of course, you can always get new jobs." Blanch knew neither of the spoiled children wanted to actually work. They liked being able to spend as they wished without any obligation to earn it. Blanch suspected the younger sister spent way more than her brother, and with a simple credit bureau check, it was confirmed both of them were in debt for over two million dollars each.

"I am prepared to buy all your shares in the business. If you are willing to sell, you can walk away clean and clear of the company's obligations." Quietly she waited for their processing of the offer to end. Six million to each of them would ensure she had controlling interest in the company, and there would be nothing Joanne could do. The sale couldn't be forced without a majority vote.

Joanne would know there would be severe implications to her own personal fortune if she weren't careful. Blanch sensed Joanne had invested well on her own through the years, and this course of action would not leave her homeless. Blanch knew it was Joanne who had built the business; Bob was just a nice man who knew how to schmooze customers.

With the children's agreement to sell, Joanne returned from her vacation to find life very different from what she had left. With her kids aligning on the side of greed, there was little she could do but accept Blanch had won round one.

An offer was made to buy Joanne's shares. The afternoon of negotiating repayment of the house as part of the deal went quite smoothly for Joanne. After she disclosed her relationship with Tessa, Blanch began to push back until Joanne let it slip that she had Gabriel's contact information and was planning to visit him in the near future. Blanch quickly closed the deal, hoping she could force the past to stay where it belonged. Nothing was mentioned about her daughter, but Blanch could not be sure who knew the true relationship between her and Kimberlee.

Kimberlee

CHAPTER 6

Kimberlee cried out for Blanch every day for several weeks after she left. At her young age, she didn't understand the connection or sense of loss and would never recover from the feeling of abandonment.

Lydia did all she knew to do to reduce the suffering Kimberlee endured. Attempts to help the toddler move past the feelings of inadequacy appeared futile. The feeling of not being good enough manifested itself in fits of rebellion toward her mom.

Lydia kept the secret to herself about Kimberlee's origin. She often thought it would be best to tell the young girl the truth. Perhaps the information would alleviate the misunderstood feelings of abandonment that were deep-seated in the young girl. She reasoned that when Kimberlee was old enough to understand, the truth would be revealed. For now, the charade would continue even though the angst within Kimberlee grew deeper in her soul as she aged.

The only other person to know the truth about her DNA was the woman known to Kimberlee as Nanna. Within a few months of Blanch's departure, her Nanna died, leaving Kimberlee to deeply feel the two losses. The outcome created a tremendous burden on her psyche, leaving her to unknowingly fear losing her mother as well.

The young girl often had vague dreams of her grandmother, reminding her of the love she garnered from the aged woman. The dreams somewhat assuaged her feeling of being cast aside. Her dreams never included the sister who left her behind; they were always of her Nanna and a man she didn't know.

Starting school, Kimberlee wasn't aware her dark skin tone made her stand out from the other children. It never occurred to her that her skin tone was off-putting to the parents of the fair-skinned children she studied next to. It wasn't until she asked her mother what a Negro was, did she begin to realize she was different from everyone else in her small town.

Her coloring, slightly darker than the maids who worked at the housekeepers' service, was a deep mocha. Most of the women who worked with her mother were Latina and carried a soft coconut shell skin tone. She often heard them referred to as "The Mexicans." She didn't know what that meant but inherently knew it was not a compliment. One woman who worked with Lydia noticed Kimberlee's dark skin and took it upon herself to advise Lydia what her daughter needed in terms of skin and hair care. The woman, being of Caribbean descent, shared her knowledge of how to care for skin with a high level of pigmentation. This would be a godsend for the mother and daughter, as Kimberlee's skin would remain flawless throughout her teenage years.

When Kimberlee asked her mother the question of race, Lydia reminded the young girl of the friend at work who taught them how to care for her skin. Lydia's approach to the subject was delivered from a clinical standpoint. She hoped to avoid the difficult conversation of race and prejudices. She explained to her young child that skin color resulted from pigmentation and had nothing to do with a person's intellect or personality. Singing the Sunday School verse to Kimberlee, "Red and yellow, black and white, they are precious in his sight. Jesus loves the little children of the world," she reminded the young girl everyone is the same on the inside.

This did little to help Kimberlee understand why she was different from everyone around her. When she looked in a mirror, she would mentally note how her looks were very different from these people; she appeared to be a mix of all of them. Her nose was thin and straight like the white girls she met at kindergarten, her hair straight like her mom's, not curly like the dark-skinned woman who provided skincare advice. Even "the Mexicans" had different skin colors and hair types. It bothered her deeply that she didn't belong to any one group; there was no one around who was like her. Throughout grade school and starting middle school, she struggled to find her place amongst the girls. She had so many unique qualities few people could relate to her.

Incredibly smart and mature, the giggle girls, as she called them, couldn't hold her interest for very long. Teachers were polite to her but were often aloof. Her high-grade points were all that garnered her accolades. Lydia saw the struggle and pondered if she should move the family beyond the boundaries of Palestine, perhaps to Dallas or Fort Worth.

Kimberlee was keenly aware people stared at her; she never could quite figure out why. No one dared speak unkind words or tease her, partially because she was almost always near her mother, and the town's folk knew of Lydia's relationship with Tessa's cousin. Joanne Fergus was not a woman not be trifled with and was not hesitant to assist Lydia whenever necessary.

On a trip to Dallas to shop for school clothes just before she began high school, Kimberlee left her mother's side to search for the women's restroom. Walking towards the Sanger-Harris store inside the mall, she spotted a restroom just inside the store. A woman exiting the ladies' room looked directly at Kimberlee and said, "Ni**ers aren't allowed in this lounge." Kimberlee smiled at the woman, moved past her, and through the door. The moment of courage was not out of indignation; Kimberlee was utterly unaware the old white woman was talking about her. In telling Lydia about the encounter, her mother realized she had kept her child sheltered from the cruel world for too long. She needed to explain the realities of the people in the South; she did not want her child to wind up in the wrong place at the wrong time.

Entering high school started a new journey for Kimberlee. Developing into an exotic-looking young woman would be her saving grace. Most girls at her school were unusually cruel to her; her unique looks were perceived as a threat to them. The perception wasn't directly related to the views shared in their homes at the dinner table; it was more about her winning the attention of would-be boyfriends.

On numerous occasions, Kimberlee visited the women's dean due to a fight with another girl. The Native American-Indian blood in her did not tolerate her being demeaned by anyone. Her lean frame offered her up as an easy target; the truth was she was pure muscle, often surprising the recipient of her fast-moving fist.

Unknown to Kimberlee, Lydia often received threats from the parents of the girls who mistreated her child. Despite Kimberlee's anger management issues, Lydia adored her and allowed her to stand up for herself no matter the outcome. The same native anger Kimberlee utilized to stand her ground was apparent in Lydia when she faced the people who threatened her or her child. Lydia was never violent with the people who sent the notes; her willingness to confront the bigotry head-on caused people to step back, establishing an unspoken reverence for the family over time. Lydia knew the wealthy family had her back; this knowledge provided a small amount of bravado on her part but was not the reason Lydia confronted the racism. She remembered all too well the stories her ancestors told of being harassed.

Kimberlee's fifteenth birthday was the year she exploded into full womanhood. Her high cheekbones further enhanced her near-perfect smile. One eye tooth being slightly askew provided an allure one could not explain. Her lips were full and naturally rose-colored. Her nostrils were slightly wide but perfectly offset by the thin bridge of her nose rising to two perfect eyebrows slightly darker than her hair. A tiny waist enhanced by her perfectly rounded buttocks and thighs. She was the perfect blend of her father's Spanish and African heritage and her mother's sultry frame. This was a young woman who now gleaned everyone's attention when she entered a room.

Lydia made sure not to repeat the mistakes made with her first daughter; she and Kimberlee openly discussed the sexual urges and desires growing in the teenage girl. Lydia was proactive in ensuring Kimberlee did not take the same path Blanch had. In addition to sexual activities, Lydia worried about Kimberlee's quick temper and her inability to fit in with others her age; she worried her sweet girl would become a loner just like her birth mother.

At sixteen, Kimberlee began asking questions about her father. As the conversation expanded, she connected the dots of her age in comparison to her mothers. Lydia struggled with how best to answer this particular question, fearing Kimberlee would react negatively. If she felt Lydia had hidden everything from her, her anger might overtake logic. One thing life had taught Lydia was the truth always reveals itself.

Driving to the grave of her mother one Sunday afternoon with Kimberlee in tow, Lydia took the opportunity to reveal her child's origin. As the story unfolded, Kimberlee sat very quietly, taking in all the information. Lydia confessed the only thing she knew of the father was his name, Gabriel Laverde. After saying his name out loud, Lydia added that she didn't know where he was now.

Kimberlee asking why her birth mother didn't want her broke Lydia's heart. To tell this beautiful child her birth mother's selfish nature was all that mattered to her seemed cruel but necessary.

Lydia continued sharing the secrets of the past, revealing to Kimberlee that it was Blanch who had given birth to her. Receiving the news without issue, Kimberlee didn't react one way or the other, merely listened to the information. Arriving home that evening, the pair moved forward with their day-to-day routines as if nothing had changed.

In the summer before Kimberlee's senior year in high school, she was somber after learning the truth of her birth. Lydia wasn't quite sure what to make of the melancholy young girl now living with her. It appeared to Lydia by telling the truth to her daughter; they had both been freed from an unknown evil driving them. The revelation gave Lydia peace of mind she had not known since before Blanch was born.

Reading a book under the open window in her bedroom, Kimberlee received a peck on the forehead as Lydia told her daughter goodnight. "I love you, my sweet; always remember you are my joy!" On that summer's eve, kissing her sweet daughter on the forehead before going to bed was her last act of physical affection to her child.

When Kimberlee woke the next morning, she sensed something was wrong; leaving the soft chair where she had fallen asleep reading her book, she went to her mother's bedroom. Laying perfectly still in her bed, a simple smile on her lips was a confirmation to Kimberlee that her mother died peacefully. Kimberlee accepted the death with tears rolling down her cheeks. Crossing to her mother, she knelt beside the bed and kissed Lydia on the forehead before saying a prayer wishing her well on her next journey.

Lydia often shared her ancestral beliefs with her child, instilling the thought in her that death was not an ending but a new beginning. Saying goodbye to Lydia, Kimberlee opened the desk drawer where Lydia kept her personal information. She looked for the little address book where Lydia's important phone numbers were kept. As she had hoped for, the first page had a number for an emergency contact. Leaving her mother peacefully in her bed, Kimberlee walked down the hallway, picked up the phone mounted on the kitchen wall, and dialed the number.

Introducing herself to the man on the other end of the line, she explained the reason for her call; her mother had passed in her sleep. She didn't cry when sharing the news; she was un-characteristically calm and sedate. The man on the other end of the phone asked her to stay where she was; he would shortly be on his way to their home. Kimberlee agreed to his request and hung up the phone's handset before returning to her room. Dressing in suitable clothes for a funer-al, she began to prepare herself for an unknown future.

When the knock on the door occurred two and a half hours later, Kimberlee answered it wearing a simple black dress and shoes. As she opened the door, she assumed the man on the front porch was the man she had spoken with on the phone. She was confident the stranger was he as they rarely had visitors that summer.

The lawyer from Dallas entered the house and introduced himself. Asking where Lydia was,

Kimberlee escorted him down the hallway to Lydia's bedroom. Lydia laid out in her best pink suit, was exactly as the man remembered her. He assumed the young girl had dressed her mother in her favorite outfit. After asking several questions, he moved to the living room and called the police and local mortuary service before calling the local newspaper.

A policeman arrived, asking a few questions to both of them; he suggested it appeared to be natural causes. Paying his respects to Kimberlee, he excused himself while Garret read the prepared obituary over the phone to a clerk somewhere across town. Kimberlee sat quietly at the kitchen table while he addressed the comings and goings of the funeral home staff.

After Lydia had been taken away on the gurney, the handsome attorney sat down across the table from the young girl and asked if she had eaten. Kimberlee thought for a moment before acknowledging she had not had any food that day and was not hungry. Assuming she was in shock, he took control of the situation, asking her what she would like to eat. A short amount of time later, the two were seated in a small restaurant ordering food. Word had traveled fast in the small town; Kimberlee sensed everyone staring at her just as the people in Dallas had done. This time she understood the reason.

Making small talk while drinking a vodka martini, the barrister attempted to comfort Kimberlee. Even though Lydia had retained him to handle her legal matters when Kimberlee was around five years old, he had never met the young girl. He was aware of her true past and who her birth mother was. He had been given specific instructions not to tell Kimberlee unless she specifically asked.

As a closeted gay man, Garret Richards had no sexual interest in the young girl but found himself staring at her beauty. He assessed that within another five years, she would be stunning beyond compare to the women he knew in his wife's powerful circle of friends. Lost in his thoughts of how this young woman would blend in with the social circle of Dallas, he was caught off guard when Kimberlee spoke. "Do you know how I can find my father?"

The question was a surprise, and he did not know how to react. Lydia had never given him instructions regarding the birth father. He wasn't sure what to say. "Mom and I recently discussed my birth. She told me his name. Do you think we can find him?" Kimberlee looked longingly into his eyes, attempting to convey her hope she might meet the man who sired her.

"I am not privy to who he is or was, but I am sure we can hire someone to help us find him." The response was not a lie, and he was somewhat relieved that Kimberlee hadn't gone into details about her birth mother.

"I have many things I need to go over with you, but first and foremost, we need to manage your mother's funeral." His lawyer-like speech took her by surprise. It was at this moment she began to release the tears for the loss of the woman who reared her.

Escorting her from the restaurant, he led her to the front seat of the car before returning to pay the bill for their supper. Apologizing to the waitress for their abrupt exit, he left a very gracious gratuity. Entering the driver's seat of the Lincoln Town Car, he found she was now sobbing uncontrollably. He did not want to take the next step but was fully aware he had no choice.

Leaving the restaurant parking lot, he proceeded towards the funeral home while Kimberlee released her sadness. Pulling into the parking lot in front of the chapel, he began speaking to Kimberlee. "Everything for the service was planned in advance by your mom. I need to make sure it is all as she requested. I would appreciate your input as well. Are you up to coming inside and seeing what has been prepared before anyone visits?"

Kimberlee nodded yes and opened the car door before stepping out onto the gravel surface. Passing in front of the car, Kimberlee took hold of her new friend. She walked stoically into the funeral parlor to see Lydia for the last time. The young woman was very pleased with how perfectly they had laid the kind woman out. The pink suit Lee had put on her mother had been removed and pressed; seeing Lydia in the crisp outfit made Kimberlee smile.

She would not attend the funeral of the woman who raised her. She couldn't bare the thought that no one would attend to bid Lydia goodbye and wanted to remember her exactly as she left her. It was unfortunate she made this choice; as many people, some as far away as Dallas, attended the service. People in the community knew of Lydia's commitment to her child and paid their respects in honor of her character.

Her final goodbye to the woman she knew as her mother was delivering her ashes to the woods on the land Lydia grew up on. She remembered the ritual from Nanna's death and did her best to repeat it fully. The lawyer in attendance cried seeing the young girl perform the ritual with such care.

Returning back to the place Kimberlee knew as home, she had many questions for the lawyer as he outlined Lydia's bequest. Going over the details, she was overwhelmed to hear all the planning Lydia had put into place to protect her.

She was also shocked to learn what she thought to be true was, indeed, not. The loss of her beloved companion shifted her perspective.

Kimberlee spent her days as a Senior in high school going to class and then returning home. She opted to finish high school living alone in the only home she ever knew. Now seventeen, the courts deemed her old enough to make this choice provided she remained in school and completed her education.

She had lost all desire to socialize even though any boy she met flirted with her. She altered her clothing style to be simple, elegant, and chic. Simple earrings with very little makeup enhanced her natural beauty. Just as her birth mother did, Kimberlee had a unique appeal about her. With the inheritance of her father's naturally toned body and skin color, she didn't need any embellishments to stand out in a crowd. She was quietly coming into her own.

Polite to the teens she went to school with, she kept them at bay. She would not forget the cruelty they had put upon her but had softened her disdain for them after hearing of the large turnout for Lydia's funeral.

Kimberlee spent her free time away from school studying, reading, and taking in the knowledge offered by the books that lined Lydia's bookshelves. Books of introspection and healing alongside literary greats. Books that would allow her insight into maturing emotionally.

She realized and came to believe the foolishness of youth should be gently put away in Pandora's box and never revisited.

CHAPTER 7

When Lydia's mother died, Lydia sought advice from someone she trusted to handle her mom's estate as well as make plans for Kimberlee's future. Unsure of the process and wary of the people in her hometown, she made a phone call to Dallas seeking help. The young girl she helped through the difficult time of her mother's murder and her father's subsequent prison term now lived in Dallas. Her job as a commercial real estate broker made her the only logical choice Lydia could think of to help with the sale of the recently inherited farmland. Lydia was unaware that Tessa's husband was also starting his new profession as a lawyer. With both of their businesses in start-up mode, Tessa and her husband were thankful to Lydia for the opportunity. Tessa didn't want to manage the sale of Lydia's family property far away from Dallas. The thought of executing a transaction from that distance concerned her; Tessa's gentle husband reminded her of the kindness and care Lydia provided in her darkest days. Tessa could not deny the request.

Lydia had been a stabilizing factor in Tessa's staying in her home while she completed high school. Her senior year and her life in utter madness, Lydia made sure Tessa knew she had someone she could lean on while Joanne Fergus was doing her best to help the young girl. Joanne often said that Lydia stepping up made the transition much smoother. Joanne often wondered why the woman was so attentive to her cousin; she was also curious why Lydia's teenage daughter did not appear to participate in the family unit. Being the same age as Tessa, Joanne assumed the girls knew each other from school. Whatever Lydia's reasoning, Joanne was thrilled to have the help.

After graduation, Lydia assisted Tessa in closing up the house she was reared in before her move to Dallas. Tessa did not want to sell the home full of memories and assumed her father would want to return to his family home after serving his prison sentence. Even though such a sad moment in her life, she didn't hate her father for killing her mother. Growing up, she knew a different man, and although she never visited him, she hoped he would find peace for what he had done. Attending Southern Methodist University, working towards a degree in business, she opted to pursue a career in commercial real estate after graduation.

Although the farm was not technically commercial property, Tessa oversaw everything for Lydia as requested. In parallel with the sale, Tessa's husband created a trust and a will for Lydia to ensure her wishes would be met at the time of her passing. Lydia was adamant the estate would pass to Kimberlee upon her death, with Garret as trustee. Blanch would receive a small stipend, mitigating the opportunity for her to contest Lydia Murrel's last will and testament.

The family land, which had provided so well for them by its use of tenant farming, was eventually sold to developers. The rapidly growing town had begun to annex land once far away from its border. It was just a matter of time before the land would be within the city limits. The developer was quick to purchase the land at a premium, knowing the rural land would have a greater value once it was within the town's boundaries. The significant amount of cash from the sale was then well invested on Lydia's behalf. Kimberlee had no knowledge of these financial arrangements Lydia was making, only that the land where they laid Nanna to rest was no longer theirs. By her eighteenth birthday, the trust left to her would carry a net value exceeding two million dollars.

Completing high school was bittersweet for Kimberlee; everything she had known was now altered. Having not reached her eighteenth birthday, Kimberlee relied heavily on her trustee to guide her.

Garret traveled back and forth from Dallas to Palestine once a week. This repeated road trip became a nice break away from his complicated life. He enjoyed his time with Kimberlee and was excited to see her blossoming and letting go of her past. The maturity she presented was astonishing to him. When initially meeting her, he sensed the information she would garner on her eighteenth birthday would be poorly received; now, having spent time with her, he felt she would handle the news without a complete meltdown.

Arriving at the house in Palestine, he observed the family car was not in the driveway. Kimberlee was aware Garret was coming for their weekly meeting. Suddenly he had an inkling something was amiss. Parking the Town Car in the street to avoid blocking the driveway, he moved up the sidewalk to the front porch of the house where Kimberlee grew up. He rapped on the door and was not surprised when no response was made. Settling into the slightly worn wicker rocking chair with its western motif fabric, he began to ponder his concern. Just as he began to dose off while rocking in the warm summer afternoon air, he heard the car make its turn into the driveway.

Kimberlee exited the well-worn Oldsmobile, apologizing for being late. "I stopped at the post office to close Mom's PO Box. I didn't even know she had one until the renewal notice came in the mail this morning." Garret was now wide awake; he had never been made aware Lydia had a post office box. He was not sure he would have the necessary details to answer any questions that might come from the correspondence held within the box. Standing up from the rocking chair, he took the other parcels Kimberlee carried while offering to review the letters she had retrieved and respond to them as appropriate. Kimberlee held on to them.

Denying his request to view them, she said, "There is so much I don't know about the woman who raised me, and it seems like some details are being withheld from me."

The only response Garret could make was to smile. Kimberlee hit the nail on the head; he had a lot of information to share with her. His directive was only to reveal the information after she was eighteen and could make legal decisions as she saw fit. He knew if she so chose, the trust would be absolved, and this young, innocent girl would be left to her own devices. Knowing what he had to tell her, he feared the maturity she had achieved would revert to her anger challenges of youth. He now wondered why he had agreed to manage the trust after he learned the ugly truth. He had information that even his wife did not know. Although he couldn't imagine his wife would care, he dreaded bringing up the name of Blanch Murrel to either of them.

Kimberlee sifted through the letters she had picked up at the post box. Each one opened, read, then handed to Garret. Hope was developing that nothing significant was within the batch of postmarked envelopes. Keeping his poker face without inflection, he quietly took each piece and reviewed it judiciously. Nothing of consequence had appeared thus far.

The teapot began to whistle; Kimberlee moved from her chair at the kitchen table towards the stove to prepare their drinks. By chance, she knocked one of the letters to the floor as she rose from the table. The envelope landing face up revealed its postmark from South America; her friend and lawyer audibly gasped. Observing the look on his face, the insightful young girl knew this was a letter of importance. She stooped down to retrieve it before returning to her chair, ignoring the whistling kettle. Her trustee had never shown any emotion beyond a kind smile; the concern expressed by his raised eyebrows confirmed there was more to her life than anyone dared tell.

Reading the letter from Gabriel, Kimberlee began to weep. His letter of condolence was not the cause of her tears, although she was touched by the kind words he wrote about Lydia. Her tears were angst from having confirmation that her mother lied to her about knowing how to reach her father. She immediately began to wonder what other truths were unknown and unspoken in the home where she lived. Looking up at the man she considered a friend as he crossed the linoleum floor to silence the screeching kettle, she asked the question he feared answering.

Pouring the hot water into the pitcher to steep the tea bags, he stared away from her. His plan had always been to partake in a few cocktails before delivering the information he had been directed to give. Bouncing the bags filled with tea leaves up and down in their hot water, he began to tell her of the past that had been kept secret from her. News of how she cried for weeks on end when her "sister" left, feeling as if she had forgotten her. The reason behind the attachment to this white girl who chose not to raise her. Information surrounding how she was conceived and used as a tool of manipulation by her birth mother. The reasons why her father hadn't taken her or initially provided for her financially or emotionally. The choice made by a middle-aged woman to raise a bastard child as her own instead of letting her go to an orphanage, where her life would have been uncertain.

By the time the iced tea arrived in front of her, Kimberlee had stopped crying. Now looking up at the man in her kitchen, a knowing smile was on her lips. "It was done out of love, wasn't it?" Kimberlee had matured enough to acknowledge the real reason behind the deceit.

"I have much more to tell you but was sworn to withhold the information until your birthday when you could, without any encumbrance from myself or anyone else, make your own choices for your future life." Reaching out to touch her shoulder, he resolved to break his promise and give her all the information during this visit. It seemed cruel to him that she would wait until the anniversary of her birth to hear the truth due her.

Moving to the phone to call his wife, he spun the rotary dial of the black metal phone hanging on the wall. He waited for Tessa to answer. He informed her he would arrive home later than initially thought as his plans had been altered. Tessa read between the lines, hung up the phone, and moved on with her day.

Kimberlee sat quietly reviewing the details of Lydia's Will & Testament. It was explained to her it still required probate, but as the law allowed, he would submit the paperwork when she reached the legal age to act on her own behalf. The process was straightforward; Lydia's assets would become a part of the trust that Kimberlee would soon control if she chose to. She questioned if she had to take control or if he would still manage it for her. "That is completely up to you. There are tax benefits to leaving the assets as they are, but nothing will stop you from dissolving the trust if you so choose."

Learning she had 2.6 million dollars sitting in various investment accounts overwhelmed her. She did not feel prepared to manage that sum of money and had no clue what was appropriate. Garret was thankful she didn't gloss over and immediately think about how to spend it. "Your birth mother could contest the will if she is aware of her mother's death, but I assume she doesn't know. I recommend we process the documents quietly to avoid any challenges. With the small amount of money awarded to her, there is little danger of her altering Lydia's wishes should she challenge the will. My colleagues at the firm agree with me there will be unnecessary legal fees should she pursue the matter."

"Do you get paid to manage the trust?" Kimberlee asked directly, which caught her trustee entirely off guard.

"I do not charge for my time but do bill the hourly rate for any clerks processing paperwork. As I understand it, your mom was a great help to my wife after her mother died. It is the least I can do, and in all transparency, I enjoyed the time spent getting to know your mom. She truly was a gift from the heavens."

"Unlike my birth mother?" There was a smirk on Kimberlee's face; he couldn't tell the reason behind the grin. "I didn't know her, so I cannot say," was all he responded.

Kimberlee asked the attorney to come back in one week. She wanted time to process everything and determine her options. She also requested he tell her whom to discuss the tax impact of her various choices. Garret suggested she come to Dallas and meet the people in charge of her trust and ask all the questions she might have.

As Garret prepared to leave for home, Kimberlee hugged him and then looked him square in the eye. "Mom had already told me about Blanch birthing me. I just thought you should know."

Garret now understood why Kimberlee had been so sanguine with the information he gave her.

Meetings were arranged, and when Kimberlee arrived in Dallas the following week, she felt she knew what she wanted to do. Tessa insisted she stay in the bungalow by their pool as she didn't like the idea of the young girl being alone in a hotel. Kimberlee had been to Dallas before, but Tessa felt she might easily be manipulated. 1980s Dallas was a bit of a wild place. Tessa recalled how quickly she got lost in it all when she arrived as a young woman. Kimberlee was thankful for the accommodations and in complete awe of the home she would reside in for the next few days.

Meeting with the trustees and accountants was quite taxing for the young girl. Lydia never discussed money with her, so this was all foreign. Monetary needs had been effortless at home, she requested what she needed or wanted, and it was either provided or denied. It was always easy. Now real-world applications applied. The accounting class she attended in high school gave her an understanding of money, but the tax law and estate management information was a bit confusing to her. The men guarding her money did their best to explain the scenarios in laypeople's terms. At times, she felt as if they were being condescending due to her age. Garret sensed her frustration, intervening when appropriate.

By the end of the three-day visit, Kimberlee had decided what she wanted going forward. Still unable to implement her choices without agreement from Garret, she shared her wishes with the team.

With her mother's passing and all the events in her life over the past year, Kimberlee had not bothered to apply to any universities. She wasn't sure if she wanted to attend college in the future, but it certainly was not going to happen soon. With that thought in her head, she requested the home she grew up in be sold. She wanted the money from the sale set up in a separate account that she could access without discussing the fund's use with anyone else. She would pack the things she wanted to keep, and all the rest would be sold or given away.

When questioned where she would live, she simply replied that she didn't know. Her first step was to discover where Gabriel was; she wanted to meet her father.

Her last request to her legal team was to alter her name. Going forward, she would use her father's last name. "I am to be called Lee Laverde from this moment on."

Lee's eighteenth birthday quietly passed, the will was probated, and the only home she ever knew was sold. All the paperwork processed and completed, her wishes were fulfilled as requested.

It was time for Lee to move forward with a new life.

CHAPTER 8

Gabriel had mellowed through the years and regretted his dismissal of the child he had unwillingly sired. Looking back, he couldn't help but feel he should have made an effort to meet his daughter. When he first reached out to Lydia ten years prior, he had no expectations of what would transpire. He did not hang hope for a response but was overjoyed when the first photo of his little girl arrived. He immediately saw the genetic influence of her Spanish and African heritage and was intrinsically proud of the beautiful child he fathered, even if not by choice.

Lydia wrote to Gabriel once a quarter without Kimberlee's knowledge, sharing the goings on in his daughter's life. It was important to her he know every event in Kimberlee's life, the good and the bad. This interaction allowed him a view of his child from a distance. Each time he received correspondence from her, he would swell with pride while observing the amazing young woman Kimberlee was becoming. When the letter from the lawyer's office in Texas arrived, he instinctively knew Lydia had passed before he even opened the envelope. Written by Garret, he made a point of letting Gabriel know provisions were in place for the future of his offspring.

Gabriel had prepared for this day and hoped his daughter would forgive him for his abandonment and make an effort to meet him. He was aware Kimberlee had little knowledge of her lineage, and he did not like the fact she had been denied her heritage. He did, however, acknowledge that by the time he decided to expose the past, his child was old enough that the damage to her and the family would be devastating. He did not want to be the cause of any more pain to her. With Lydia's passing, the truth was available to the young woman; the choice for her future involvements was ultimately hers; Kimberlee could decide her own path.

Time passed slowly for Gabriel after learning Lydia had died. He was unsure what he should do for his daughter if anything. The answer appeared in a letter that arrived in mid-October that same year. Gabriel had not expected this turn of events. Its contents outlined his daughter's desire to meet him at least once. Kimberlee's, nay now simply Lee, trustees were unsure how the young girl would manage in a world she knew little about. They feared for her safety and the possibility she might squander away her inheritance. Gabriel immediately phoned the attorney in Dallas, confirming his desire to meet his child.

Upon her return to Palestine from Dallas to finalize her plans to exit the land she had known since birth, Lee began making the necessary arrangements for a trip to South America. In addition to applying for a passport, Lee visited her physician to make sure she was ready for the trip to a third-world country. She was clueless about what lay beyond the borders of the United States. By the time the American Thanksgiving holiday arrived, Lee was on a plane bound for Cartagena, Columbia. Landing in a foreign country with no knowledge of its language or currency, Lee was overwhelmed emotionally. Her anxiety over how she would manage her life outweighed the nervousness about meeting her father.

Gabriel waited patiently at the airport gate for his child. As she exited the plane, she saw a man she had never met but knew immediately he was her dad. An instant connection between the two of them formed when their eyes met. Resembling the man standing at the gate, she knew she looked enough like him to confirm he was Gabriel. Her looks mainly had come from her father; only her exceptionally light green eyes and straight western nose reflected her mother. Observing the neatly tucked-in shirt and extremely fitted pants, Gabriels' beautiful frame was revealed to her. A body she recognized, a body looking back at her each time she looked in the mirror. Lee made a mental note to thank him for passing on the family's shapely features.

Reaching the bottom of the stairs onto the tarmac, Lee began a quick pace toward the man she was there to meet. Gabriel hoped for a hug but extended his hand to shake hers, just in case she was not ready. Quickly crossing the firm black pavement, she saw his hand extend. The implied proper greeting did not dissuade her from throwing her arms around his neck and kissing him on the cheek. He returned the kiss to her cheek in proper European fashion, first left, then right. Lee didn't understand this ritual, but it didn't matter to her. She was in a new world with her father, on her way to finding a family she desperately needed.

Lee was graciously welcomed by her new family. Her uncle, whom she recognized from Texas, was first to greet her when they entered the room. "We have met on one or two occasions during your childhood; please know I never knew you were family until your mother passed. I am sorry for your loss."

Gabriel confirmed that no one except Lee's birth mother, Lydia, Nanna, and he knew the truth of her past. Taking Lee's hands into his, he looked at her appreciatively. "I have saved all the letters Lydia sent. I hope we can go through each of them together; I want you to share your life with me and fill in the blanks of what I missed."

Lee began to look pensive. Gabriel was concerned he had pushed too hard, too soon. Lee pulled her hands free from her father's grip. "I will share small bits with you, but that is a life built on lies. I loved my mom, Lydia, but have no interest in spending energy on an inauthentic life." Lee smiled sweetly at Gabriel, hoping he understood her intent was to focus on the future; he did.

Christmas quickly came and passed. Lee experienced many new cultures and customs, rituals which oddly felt natural to her as if she had grown up participating in them. Generational activities provided her with details of her inner being that had been missing. There was a deep connection to her ancestors that she never knew existed. Growing up in Texas, the rituals Lydia shared with Lee were the typical Anglo-Saxon holiday themes of Christmas. Native observances Lydia grew up with were also shared in a limited fashion. Combining the new cultures with the old, the holiday created a wholeness in Lee she had not expected. The childhood issues of feeling unwanted had begun to melt away. She was finding her story.

As the new year approached, discussions about how long she would remain in Columbia began. Government requirements needed to be addressed if she intended to stay in South America. Lee stated she wanted to stay for at least six months to enhance her sense of their way of life. Gabriel agreed upon one condition; she must attend university. "My home is in Cali; the Universidad del Valle is there. We will have you enrolled promptly as an international student while you decide if you want to stay here long-term." Gabriel did not want to force any decisions on his child; he feared she was strong-willed and, if pushed, would react as he did when he was young. Meeting her now reminded him of his limited focus at her age. He didn't want to lose the opportunity to spend time with her but would leave that for her to decide. She readily agreed to his conditions.

"Bueno, esto está decidido. ¡Mañana, nuestros iremos a mi casa!" Gabriel watched Lee and her response to his having spoken in Spanish. She appeared to be processing the words that flowed out from his lips.

"I got tomorrow and, I think, my home. You said we will leave for your home in Cali tomorrow?" Looking at her dad for confirmation her interpretation was correct, Lee appeared a bit sheepish.

"Good, you at least know a few words. People will expect you to be fluent in Spanish. Now that you carry the Laverde name, they will assume you speak proper Castilian." He knew his daughter was in for a challenge; he hoped she could rise to the occasion over the long haul.

The first semester she attended Universidad del Valle, Lee struggled with her classes. Most of the professors spoke several languages, and when she struggled with context or correct word order, they would correct her in English with the proper use. Her fellow students attempted to use their limited knowledge of English to help her out as well. Her beauty and her last name carried a lot of weight within the city. Her skin coloring was also helpful; she was not perceived as a white child attempting to alter their way of life.

As the end of the school year approached, Gabriel's legal team connected with Garret. Together, they worked their magic and obtained a student visa for her to remain through the summer courses. By the end of her extended tour visiting her father, Lee had accomplished the task of being bilingual. Gabriel did not consider her fluent but well-versed enough to survive without him. He often worried his American daughter would catch the attention of FARC members, leaving her vulnerable if on her own. He did not share his concern with Lee; he feared the knowledge of the organization would push her to leave him. Gabriel focused on keeping her with him or at school and demanded, if asked where she was from, she would reply her family lived in Madrid.

As summer school was nearing its end, Lee had to decide what her next path would be. Her visa would not allow her to stay in the country if she didn't continue attending school. She didn't believe she belonged there long term; she felt something was still missing from her life. Sharing this information with her father over dinner one night, he said he understood and encouraged her to visit other countries. "Go to Spain and meet your cousins, tour France and Asia, and search for the place you believe is your future home. You have so much going for you; see how far it will take you."

Seeking input from her friends at university, Lee conceded her father was correct. She didn't want to return to the States just yet. She had the means to explore for a year or two before asking for trust money, so why not. Gabriel made the necessary phone calls to the correct family members in Madrid. Lee would have family and emotional assistance when she arrived overseas.

Gabriel did not mention to his daughter or his family overseas his recent diagnosis of Alzheimer's disease; he had a plan to deal with his future. His daughter had brought him the happiness he had been seeking, and this gave him solace that his plan to end his life was the right choice.

Arriving in Madrid that fall, Lee was met at the seaport by her cousin Ernesto. He was polite to her, speaking English as he had been told she was an American. He appeared irritated by her being there; she began questioning whether going there had been a good choice. Her father had encouraged her to go; he strongly felt, with all his heart, that being around her blood family would be what she needed to find the next course in her journey. The picture he had painted in her mind did not match the reality of what she was walking into.

Arriving at Pozuelo de Laverde, Lee was surprised to see the grand estate where her distant family lived. Moving towards the front gates, her peripheral vision saw her newly acquired last name etched into the stone markers on each side of the gate. This was truly something unexpected. She also noticed the black bows and sashes spread across the face of each gate as it swung backward away from the nose of the Mercedes she was riding in. It dawned on her that the young man who retrieved her from the seaport had been less than pleasant because the family must be in mourning, and she was intruding on their grief.

Pulling under the Porte Cochère, she was met by three beautiful women of differing ages. They appeared to her as a generational gathering led by the family matriarch. Stepping from the car, she was greeted by each of them with a kiss on each cheek. She now knew how to return the greeting appropriately. The eldest of the group greeted her last, and after the official greeting, she pulled Lee into an unexpected hug. Releasing Lee from the embrace, the matriarch expressed a thought in Spanish. The flow and timbre were spoken fast and low; Lee only caught a few words. She made out the words for my dear and death, nothing else. Just as she feared, she had arrived amid a family crisis. Lee's lack of reaction caused the matriarch to step back from the young American girl with a stunned look on her face. She turned to the other women and the man who drove Lee from the port and spoke. The young man responded in English to Lee, "Are we to gather you have not received the terrible news?"

Lee turned to the young man and shook her head no. She had no idea what he was speaking about or how it might involve her. "I truly have no clue what you are talking about."

Ernesto turned to the women and spoke quickly, relaying his message with a rushed intent. Lee felt this was on purpose; she sensed they were avoiding giving her information. Feeling at a loss, she stepped beyond the car and sat down on a bench near the stone path. Conversations continued between the family members while they looked directly at her. The youngest of the women asked if Lee needed something to drink. "Si, gracias. Agua, por favor."

The ladies quickly congregated while moving toward the side door of the house; they were soon out of sight. Lee could still hear them talking as they walked away. The young man, whom she had assumed to be her cousin, walked behind the bench and sat next to her.

Taking her hand into his, Ernesto looked into her eyes before speaking. A soft sphere of moisture on the edge of his right eye began trailing down his cheek as he began to share with her, "I am sorry to be the one to deliver this informa-

tion to you. Your father died in a boating accident
day before yesterday."

CHAPTER 9

Days moved by very quickly, Lee losing count of how many had passed since she arrived in Spain. Nothing had prepared her for the emotions spewing from within after receiving the news of Gabriel's death. It was all so sudden, leaving her overwhelmed by the vast amount of sadness consuming her. She had only known Gabriel for less than a year; she couldn't comprehend why there was such a connection between the two. The impact on her was at par with the loss of the woman who raised her. This unexpected event added to the layers of sadness she struggled to move past on a daily basis.

Gabriel's extended family was surprisingly gracious to her, offering her an invitation to stay with them until she was ready to go. In this time of grief, it never occurred to any of them that Lee was a visitor in Spain, and immigration should have been notified about her staying on.

Lee and her English-speaking cousin, the man who had delivered the bad news to her, had begun to grow close. As each day passed, the love blossoming between them was platonic and would bond them forever. Ernesto's boyfriend, Tino Alvarez, was enjoyable to be around as well, for the most part. Lee enjoyed his antics but quickly recognized he was definitely a handful to deal with.

The three of them spent most days enjoying the offerings of Madrid while enjoying each other's company immensely. The boys taught Lee things she would have never had the opportunity to learn in Texas. Even the socialites in the pretentious city of Dallas could not have given her the insight she gained from her two new best friends. They taught her European ways of dressing, how to wear her hair and makeup, and the right dress to wear based on the event. Ernesto explained European etiquette to Lee, going so far as to show her the right fork to use at dinner. She adapted quickly to the social aspects of international society; it was as if her genetic background had found its perfect soil to take root in.

By the time the Ministry of Migration caught up with her, Lee was cultured in the ways of Europe. She was fully prepared to move to another country and find her way.

Now in her twenties, Lee had become confident in herself and the woman she was becoming. The family attorney did his best to resolve her immigration status and thus avoid her being deported. When the government denied her request for citizenship, primarily due to her overstaying her visit and not making the request upon arrival, she was given thirty days' notice to vacate the country. The government was quite lenient with her simply because of her family name; she would have the opportunity to reapply for citizenship once she was out of the country for a minimum of 180 days. The family discussed options with their lawyer and was advised it was best she did as immigration had directed. Lee should move on.

The elders of the Laverde clan reminded the family of past scandals and believed the surname could not afford another disgrace in the public eye. Confirming to the family she would leave quietly; Lee discretely asked Tino for details surrounding the "family scandal." "I don't know of anything the family keeps a secret." When she asked Ernesto, he suggested it was in her best interest not to dig into the past. He did, however, suggest the incident involved her father and was the reason for his relocation to Columbia when he was a teenage boy.

Preparing to leave, Tino excitedly offered to assist Lee in settling somewhere new. She had no desire to return to the US, and Tino was thrilled about that decision; he was not overly fond of the Americans. When Lee questioned why, Tino changed the subject quickly.

In his travels around the world, there had been a few good times enjoyed with closeted young men in the States. The men were often bored with him and his outlandish style in a very short amount of time. The invitations to the lavish parties would stop abruptly, leaving him as nothing more than a boy toy for the bedroom. Growing tired of being sexually exploited, Tino returned to Europe. It was on the journey home he met Ernesto, who was returning to Spain after a trip to the Florida Keys. The two of them bonded over their bad experiences with American men. Lee's cousin had been the longest relationship Tino had ever endured, and after six years, he was beginning to tire of Ernesto.

The offer to go away with Lee was really one of self-want; this would provide a good reason to let things cool down with his lover before ending it for good. Tino didn't enjoy confrontation, so he steered around the conflict by using Lee as his excuse to go.

The unlikely pair discussed where she should go next. It was suggested by Tino they spend some time in France. He was fluent in French and would begin to teach her the language immediately. They reasoned that half a year would pass by quickly, then she could choose whether she wanted to return to the Pozuelo de Laverde. It took less than a week to pack the trunks for their journey; they were ready to set off on their adventure.

Phoning Garret in the States was unsettling for Lee. Updating him on her reasons for moving on to France versus returning home, Garret informed her she should return to the US before going to France for an extended period of time. France required a visa for an extended stay of an American citizen. A flight to Washington, DC, was arranged, where she met her lawyers and presented her case to return to Europe. The team agreed that capitalizing on her father's death and the necessity to visit family overseas should win sympathy from the immigration officials and probably expedite the request. Within a short amount of time, Lee had the paperwork she needed to board a plane to meet Tino in Marseille.

Tino felt the French Riviera would make a nice transition from Madrid. Most people in the city of 800,000 spoke multiple languages, which would help the learning curve for Lee. If she couldn't find the words in French, there was most likely someone who spoke English nearby who could assist. As fall approached and the coastal towns began to slow their pace, Lee requested they move on to Paris. Her appetite for fashion had been awakened; she wanted to shop on the Champs-Elysées and dine in the Latin Quarter.

Their adventure in Paris began in a hotel bar at Le Meurice. Sharing an apéritif before walking through the park on their way to dinner, Lee was approached by a handsome man. Her immediate observation of him was he was older than she by several years. His face was youthful, but his hair was silver; the juxtaposition of the two presented a charming, distinguished gentleman. "Enchanté, mademoiselle. Comment vous-appelez vous?" His voice was deep and lyrical; she was immediately taken by him. "Bonsoir, monsieur. Je m'appelle Lee, et mon ami, Tino." The silver-haired man acknowledged Tino before returning his gaze to Lee. She was surprised by this as, typically, men used her as the conduit to meet Tino. The stranger's perfect manicure and fitted waistcoat left her to assume the silver-haired man to be homosexual. Tino was not amused by the man's dismissive nature towards him. Quickly devouring his drink, he stood and requested the man excuse them as they were on their way to dinner. Lee was taken aback by how gruff Tino was towards the charming man; she felt a slight tinge of anger towards him for his behavior. The man excused himself and moved on; Tino returned to his seat and ordered another cocktail.

Walking back to the hotel after dinner, Lee asked why he had been unpleasant to the man who approached them. Tino offered no apologies, "I have to be mindful of who tries to entertain you. Many men will do their best to take advantage of a young girl of means like you." Lee mentally noted the statement. The words recalled an observation she had made a few months back about how Tino's wallet never appeared when the bill came due. She pondered how much energy she should put into exploring his behavior in more detail. While in Spain, she assumed her cousin was insistent on paying for everything, and Tino just allowed it. Now that Ernesto and the Laverde fortune were not readily available, was she expected to be on the hook for his expenses?

Lee awoke early the following day; she had not slept well. Spending the night pondering past events with Tino and attempting to reconcile her feeling of being taken advantage of left her beside herself. Unless her cousin told Tino she had money, she didn't think he could have knowledge of her inheritance. She didn't perceive the family to be of a mindset of divulging information to outsiders.

Quietly leaving the hotel suite, she made her way to the small cafe on the corner of the street facing L'Opera de Paris. Sitting at a small table in the corner, enjoying her favorite new-found morning ritual of Cafe au Lait and Croissant, she saw the elegant silver-haired man exiting the opera house. Walking up the street towards her, she made an unusually bold move and greeted him as he passed. He responded appropriately and continued on his path. Returning to her pastry, she was startled when he quietly returned and suggested he join her.

Summoning a waiter and ordering an espresso, he asked if she needed anything. She smiled and said no thank you in his native tongue. He took a seat and began a conversation with her in French. As she verbally stumbled through her responses, he concluded she was not French and asked where she was from, "España?" Her response was made in Spanish, assuming he would understand. In very broken Spanish, he shared that his language skillset was limited to French and English. Lee was thrilled to hear him say that he spoke English and responded, "Je suis américain."

They enjoyed an hour of conversation covering topics from Texas to the loss of her father. He was surprised this elegant young woman of apparent means exuded such great humility. He blatantly asked about the man she had introduced him to the evening before, "Your boyfriend, lover?" She quickly confirmed Tino was neither. Continuing on, she explained how many of the men she had met so far in Paris used her as an excuse to meet Tino, and she assumed he was doing the same. He laughed at the observation before assuring her he was a Kinsey 1 - predominantly heterosexual. Lee had never heard of this rating and wondered what "predominantly heterosexual" meant. She needed to figure that out.

As the sun rose towards its peak of the day, they were interrupted by Tino. He quickly assessed the interest between the two and apologized for his rude behavior the evening before. The men shook hands and agreed on how beautiful Lee was before Tino excused himself. Leaving them alone, Tino crossed to the cafe's doors to acquire sustenance. When he returned, the silver-haired gentleman had retreated from the patio, leaving a vacant cane chair for Tino.

"Well, that was very cozy! Why didn't you wake me this morning?" Tino posed many more questions before Lee could respond to the first one. Finally, he took a sip from his demitasse, allowing her a moment to respond. Leaving her suspicions around his behavior out of her response, she simply implied he was in a deep sleep when she looked in on him. She opted to let him rest while she had her coffee. "That was very sweet of you, thank you. So tell me, what's his name?"

The expression on her face was one of irritation; "I never asked!" Throwing her hands in the air in exasperation, she released a sigh as she spoke. "Finally meet a Kinsey 1 man, and I forget to ask him his name." Tino stopped mid-sip of his espresso and looked across the rim of his cup; he was pretty sure she didn't have a clue what her statement implied. "You know about the Kinsey Studies?" Curious to hear her thoughts, he set the cup and saucer on the table. He didn't want to spill anything should he begin to giggle at her response. Lee shook her head from side to side; it was just as he suspected. She didn't have a clue.

Walking back to the hotel, Tino explained what the studies in the 1950s had concluded and suggested that no man was a zero or a six. "What they left of their studies was how much liquor had been consumed and how long it had been since the man had any!" Lee thought his response on the subject to be a bit crass; mentally, she noted his behavior as lacking class, along with his not paying for anything at the cafe.

Before Tino returned to the table that morning, Lee's companion graciously offered to pay the bill. Lee requested he pay for his own items and left it at that. When the gentleman exited, he dropped enough francs on the table to cover his and her parts of the bill. When the check for breakfast was delivered, Tino's items had been included; he loaded the coins on the table onto the tray and rose to leave.

That evening, Lee laid out a black dress that perfectly framed her curvaceous body before climbing into a bath. After she was sufficiently refreshed from the water, she applied a touch of lipstick, pulled her hair up into a simple but elegant twist, and slid into her dress and heels. Loading the matching handbag with a few necessities, she exited her bedroom, encountering Tino on the sofa in the living area. He reviewed her appearance as stunning and said she should have given him notice to dress for dinner. As he rose from his perch, she snapped her clutch closed. "I am so sorry, I am guessing I forgot to tell you, what's his name asked me out for dinner. You are on your own this evening. Please forgive me."

Tino began to pout but quickly pulled himself together. He wished her a wonderful evening and escorted her to the hallway of the hotel. He sensed he needed to be careful about his reactions going forward. Something in the wind had shifted, and Tino could sense it. If she told him to go home anytime soon, there might be serious consequences for him. He asked her to wait for a moment and went to his room. Returning to her standing by the entrance to the room, Tino fastened a Harry Winston Wave Brooch to her slim lapel. "I've been saving this up for a special occasion, and I think tonight will certainly be one!" Lee turned to look in the mirror by the elevators admiring the stunning platinum and diamond piece of jewelry, and she smiled. The only reason she knew it was a Harry Winston piece was that it looked identical to the one her great-aunt wore to the wake for Gabriel. The woman, even though in mourning, was thrilled to tell Lee about the piece and its value. One more thing to question about her devoted male companion. Where had he acquired this expensive piece of jewelry? Tino's list of negative traits was beginning to pile up.

Exiting the elevator on the ground floor, she caught a glimpse of herself in the hallway mirrors. No one would have ever thought this woman had come from humble beginnings in rural Texas. She liked how she looked, and even though it was most likely stolen, she loved how the brooch enhanced her overall appearance. Her escort for the evening was overwhelmed by her beauty; watching her walk from the elevator toward him, he shed a tear. Seeing the drop move down his cheek, she said, "That explains why you're predominantly heterosexual and not a perfect zero." She felt very clever with her statement but was not prepared for his response. "No, mon cherie, that tear is because I am French and am always moved by a thing of beauty."

She had never felt so beautiful or been treated so delicately; Lee knew she could get used to this. Leaving the entrance to the hotel, all eyes were on the beautiful couple. Lee's exotic shape, perfectly outlined in the dress adorning her, was enhanced only by his exquisite good looks. To the casual observer, they were a perfect fit and had been together for a long time.

As he slid onto the seat beside her in the back of the Peugeot, he directed the driver to go. Arriving at their destination, she noticed the chauffeur backed the car into a spot and remained nearby after their exit from the car. The driver's job dictated he always wait for the man he served as coachman and valet.

The elegant man seated across from her at dinner asked if she needed help with the menu written in French. She replied in perfect dialect, "Non, Merci." He smiled at her, and they began to converse in his native tongue. Lee confessed that she was tired that morning and was overwhelmed by him, that her brain struggled to find the words she needed. Finally, the moment came; she needed to confess she had never asked his name. He laughed slightly, confessing he did not recall hers either, and was embarrassed to ask. Introductions were made as a bottle of red wine filled their glasses.

The evening was one of Fairy Tales, most young girls grow up wishing for; Lee realized how lucky she was to have partaken in hers.

Time in Paris passed by without warning. Experiencing the seasons change in Paris, Lee decided an apartment in the Latin quarter would be home for the near future. Winter was soon upon them, and Jacque had invited her to Switzerland, where he would teach her to ski. He was even so kind as to extend the invitation to Tino. Jacque had not fully unraveled the connection between Lee and Tino, and he wasn't sure of the man's purpose in her life. He thought it best to let the true nature of their friendship reveal itself over time. Lee never passed the invitation on to Tino; she left him at the apartment in Paris while she experienced a new aspect of life without him in tow.

Over the course of the months, since they had met, Lee and Jacque's sex life had not evolved as she had hoped. With all the ups and downs of her life, she was, for all intents and purposes, a virgin. She had participated in various forms of fellatio and mutual masturbation, but she had never been penetrated by a man. She hoped this ski trip would provide her with that missing piece of carnal knowledge she desired.

In addition to placing her on a pedestal, Jacque did not allow Lee to pay for anything, even though she often attempted to. This came to a head on their trip to Switzerland when she paid for her ski lessons with her own credit card. Lee didn't understand why he was insulted; in her mind, it showed her as an independent woman who could manage on her own. This was precisely what the issue was for him; he wanted a woman who depended on him. He wanted to be the provider, the protector, and the leader of the family unit.

Quietly sequestered in the living room of their suite at the ski lodge, Lee graciously explained to Jacque she appreciated his giving nature but that she struggled with the thought of being dependent on anyone. He requested the two of them to find a compromise that would allow him to dote on her as he saw fit while never objectifying her.

Over dinner on the last night of their trip, she overheard a couple at a table nearby speaking Spanish. Eavesdropping in an attempt to brush up on the language, she was shocked to hear their observation of her and Jacque. It was then she understood the challenge to his masculinity; the couple debated why an American heiress who looked like her would be spending time with an older man like him. Jacque internally feared how others viewed their age difference and whether she needed him or wanted him. Recognizing how this emotionally emasculated him, she happily embraced his need to spoil her.

Returning to her apartment in the 5th arrondissement, she confided in Tino that skiing wasn't the only skill she picked up in St. Moritz. Lee spent as much time with Jacque as his work schedule would allow. She even went so far as to mention her LV suitcase had a tear in it, offering him the chance to have it repaired for her. She was taken aback when a complete set of new Vuitton travel cases arrived at her apartment the following day.

Arriving at his apartment wearing a long coat and nothing but La Perla underneath, she thanked him for his kindness. Laying on the floor in front of the fire, she kissed him with reckless abandon before announcing that she completely belonged to him.

With Tino as her maid of honor, Jacque and Lee were married three months later at Pozuelo de Laverde. With the Harry Winston jewelry on her dress, Tino attempted to dissuade her from walking down the aisle with the brooch. He said it pulled focus away from her dress. It was then that she forced Tino to acknowledge he had stolen it.

Delaying the start of the wedding until he sought forgiveness from her Tia for the theft, she gave him a choice. Confess, or she would tell the family what he had done and personally disown him. The brooch removed from her gown, Tino made his way to find Ernesto and explain why the wedding was delayed. Before long, Tia Rosa entered the bride's room and pinned the jewelry on her gown. "It is with the family blessing you wear this today. This piece was a gift to Gabriel's mother on her wedding day, and now it belongs to you. You have proven yourself, my dear; by forcing a friend to do what was right, you have returned honor to your family."

Lee was slightly saddened by the fact she didn't have her Texas family, or her father, with her on the day of her wedding. She missed her mom but was sure Lydia's presence was with her. She hoped Gabriel was nearby as well.

CHAPTER 10

Being married to Jacque was more fulfilling than Lee could have ever hoped for. He was kind to her and, without question, provided anything she needed, which was nothing. Her personal estate in Texas continued to increase in value under the careful watch of her trustee. Lee only accessed her private accounts for personal expenses or when she wanted to surprise Jacque with a gift.

Garret advised her to never disclose her net worth to anyone, including her spouse. For that reason, her personal assets were a mystery to Jacque. It was her suggestion the two of them put a prenuptial agreement in place before they wed. Jacque was surprised by her request but agreed quickly, knowing his family would have pushed him to initiate one anyway. Through the life she now lived, she gained an understanding of old money. People who lived with means did not discuss financial matters outside a business deal and never bragged about what they had recently acquired. Lee had become adept at spotting a Nouveau Riche and did her best to avoid them at all costs. The irony of her avoidance did not go unnoticed by herself or Tino.

With her name altered, there were no ties back to Texas linking her to a meager upbringing, and most times, when she revealed she was from Texas, people assumed she was old oil money. After the incident in St. Moritz, she was aware people saw her as an heiress who was well-educated and understood the requirements of polite society. She mentally gave credit to Tino and Ernesto for introducing her to the finer things in life, and even though they were not together any longer, she cherished the memories of their time spent together.

After forcing Tino to return the jewelry he took from the Laverde family, the two of them came to an agreement on how they would interact in the future. Lee knew Tino needed someone to provide for him; she also recognized his ability to make things happen and guide her when she might falter. She valued him as a guide and assistant but was very cautious with what information she shared with him.

Jacque was wary of Tino and most definitely did not like him but recognized Lee needed him for personal reasons. He did not dissuade her alliance with the man, especially after gaining insight into her past. He viewed Tino as a threat to his wife and opted to use other means to manage Tino without his wife's knowledge.

Both men gained an appreciation for each other over time. Most notably, each of their ability to destroy anyone who might cause grief for the woman they cherished. Tino understood the boundaries set out by Jacque and did not dare cross them. He knew Jacque's assistant had many other talents beyond being his valet and chauffeur, and he was not willing to test the man's skill sets. In addition to Tino's fears of being found at the bottom of the Seine, the monthly deposit to his personal checking account ensured the two men were in sync where Lee was concerned.

With her marriage to Jacque, Lee was now a French citizen, which allowed her to easily travel to the neighboring countries. A high-speed train would often whisk her away from Paris, where she would visit the Laverde Clan in Madrid; Tino never joined her at Pozuelo de Laverde. His duties were to escort her across the continent and disappear when they arrived in Madrid.

The Laverde family treated her with high regard. Even with her status in the family established, no one spoke much of Gabriel and the challenges that had driven him to move away. Questions raised about her father would be answered in a benign manner with little information imparted. She wanted to know more about the man who supplied her with near-perfect features and the heritage she now enjoyed. The sister who followed him to South America died from cancer long before Lee ever met her dad; she was rarely spoken of either.

Acquiring photos of him in his youth, Lee was surprised at how much she looked like her father when he was an adolescent. As a young boy, his features were soft and feminine. He was almost womanly in the photos depending on how he was dressed. So much so she sometimes questioned his gender. She finally convinced herself his moving to South America had been the right thing for him. It allowed him to grow into a handsome man who was charming and rugged. The man who beguiled her birth mother.

When the matriarch of the Laverde family passed away, the family relaxed its propriety a small amount. After her funeral, information regarding Gabriel was finally disclosed to Lee. The true cause of his leaving for Columbia was finally revealed. The family's matriarch forbade the story to be told while she was alive. Now, with her passing, Lee's aunts and uncles felt Lee deserved to know the reasons behind her father not wanting children and his need to move away and start anew.

Tia Maria sat across from Lee with a large glass of Port in her hand as she began to share the family history. "Doña Laverde's brother was a priest. His climb toward the Vatican was fast and calculated. Loving her brother deeply, she ignored the rumors of his sexual abuse of the altar boys.

She inherently knew the rumors to be true but did nothing about it. When Gabriel came to his Abuela seeking help, she refused to talk about the incident he had encountered. We believe the guilt she carried was very difficult for her, but her faith did not allow her to question the church." Learning how the priest repeatedly abused her father was difficult for her; hearing how Gabriel ended the abuse was unimaginable.

Gabriel ended the ritual abuse by setting the man who raped him on fire while he slept. Lee certainly did not expect such an extreme level of retaliation. His actions created a media storm that began to tear the family apart. Family members were shocked to learn his grandmother had not protected the boy, choosing to allow him to suffer repeatedly.

His choice to leave Spain and start over resonated with her. Lee understood how such deep emotional damage impacts one's logical reasoning ability. The information imparted gave insight into his actions. She understood the anger he felt, the feeling of abandonment even with those who cared deeply for him nearby. His life was not dissimilar to her journey. Gaining this knowledge sparked a thought buried deep in the back of her mind. What could have happened to her mother that caused her to give Lee up at birth? Even though fate provided her with a near-perfect life, the gnawing feeling of abandonment had never left her. It was a silent monster lurking about.

Returning home to Jacque, who had remained in Paris, Lee left Tino to wander around Spain as he willed. She needed time alone with her husband, days without interruptions from her sidekick.

Back in her comfortable bed next to her husband, she said a little prayer of thanks for all that had been afforded her. She and Jacque would be heading to the Alps the following week for a ski pilgrimage. She was genuinely excited about this adventure and hoped its outcome would be fruitful.

Now in her late twenties, the desire to have a child of her own was a constant thought in the forefront of her mind. Subtly broaching the idea with her husband, Jacque welcomed the idea of having children; they willingly chose to avoid using birth control and leave pregnancy up to fate. After six years of sexual intimacy without conceiving, both of them wondered if they ever would have the pleasure of raising a child of their own. Lee knew many options to acquire a child existed, but she wasn't ready to concede just yet.

Lee's physician deemed she was perfectly capable of getting pregnant; that left an unspoken pressure on Jacque. Crawling into bed next to him in their apartment in Paris, Jacque was alive with anticipation for a night of passion. His erection was short-lived when she advised him there would be no sexual activity in the near future. Self-care was not an option either; he was to abstain from ejaculating until she began to ovulate. Lee smiled when she noticed his disappointment and quickly promised that when the timing was right, she would make it worth his suffering with morning and evening bedroom activities.

Gathering around the large open fireplace in the lodge's main room after a day of playing in the snow, an acquaintance questioned why Lee was not drinking. Lee thought the middle eastern man to be rude for asking such a question. Noticing her eyebrows slightly furrowed, he offered the pretense her lack of alcohol consumption was the reason her skin was so perfect. Relaxing her facial muscles after his explanation, she assured him it was pure genetics that blessed her with such beautiful skin. She then added a confession that she maintained a daily regimen of skincare utilizing botanicals. "You are stunning. Should you have any interest in trying my skincare line, I would be thrilled to have your honest feedback. The science behind it will only enhance your beauty. And thinking aloud, if you would endorse it, you could be a part of our new advertising campaign." The gentleman owned and operated a well-known skincare brand in the United States, which was finding much success. After he had introduced himself, she recalled seeing ads for his products in Vogue and Elle magazines; she felt his taking notice of her skin was indeed a compliment.

The timing now ideal, as promised, they returned to their bedroom that evening, where Jacque was pleasured by his wife and her deep-seated desire to collect his specimen. Lee followed all the directions she read in a book listing the best positions to conceive. Her husband was thrilled with the variety of tantric techniques she utilized.

As their trip was nearing its end, Lee expressed her disinterest in returning to Paris to Jacque. He would be busy working, leaving her to fill her days with whatever adventure Tino would suggest, assuming he had returned to France. She was tired of corner cafes and pastries, and her hopes for pregnancy elevated her desire to be useful and find a purpose.

Waking up in his arms the last morning of their trip, Jacque suggested they stay in bed and enjoy the quiet time together. The internal warmth she had lying next to him reminded her why she had fallen in love with him. His very being was in tune with her every need, and he had never disappointed her. She expected there would be difficult times in the future, as every marriage has and believed her life partner would always be committed to finding a path to resolution.

Staying very close to him that morning, she gently reached for his groin and began stroking his semi-erect manhood. Moving down his torso with her lips, she reached his navel and probed it with her tongue before taking him into her mouth. Jacque pulled her away from his hard phallus, "You are aware you can't fertilize eggs through your stomach." The slight grin on his face at the preposterous suggestion made Lee smile. She then kissed him on the lips before returning to his groin, "This is just for you, my love. Lay back and enjoy."

Completing her task, she made her way back to the top of the bed. Snuggling with her husband, she enjoyed the post-fellatio relaxed state he was in. With her pregnancy initiative in full swing, Lee intended to skip the time on the slopes with her husband that day. "Go and enjoy your last day of skiing. I will get everything prepared for the trip home. Remember, we have to leave here by 3:00 to catch the flight."

Jacque kissed his wife goodbye before snapping the skis into the locks on his boots. Sliding through the snow, he headed for the lift. Before he was out of sight, he turned back to see her watching him through the window. He blew her a kiss and then was quickly out of sight.

Lee sat down in the chair beside the fireplace and began to consume her morning latte. Daydreaming about being pregnant, she reached for a pen to begin writing down possible names for the baby. Although she wouldn't know for a few weeks if she was pregnant or not, her gut told her everything was about to change. Looking at the clock while jotting down names, she was startled to see how much of the morning she had let slip by. Laying the pen and pad down, she moved to the bedroom and began to gather their clothes for packing.

At home, Jacque had his valet manage these things. Even though she liked folding his clothes and smelling his scent on them, her husband preferred she allow the help to perform these tasks. Jacque often pushed her to hire a maid to manage her clothes and such, but she had never grown comfortable with the idea. She was just a little girl from Texas, and she knew how to care for herself very well. She paused while packing her bags and decided she would hire someone to help after the baby arrived. She felt this decision would make Jacque very happy.

After a shower and then drying her hair, she decided her coif should be pulled into a top knot. She would wear some sort of hat for the journey home; she hoped her husband wouldn't mind. She could always use the excuse they were running late if a comment was made.

Looking at the clock on her vanity, she was surprised to see it was already 2:00. Thinking to herself; he should be back by now so they could leave on time, she pursed her lips in aggravation while applying her moisturizer and lip gloss. Placing the last of her toiletries in her bag, she zipped it up and began to pack his Dopp kit. "He will have to travel without a clean shave," she spoke out loud to herself.

Another glance at the clock, it was now 2:35. She looked around the dressing area and resigned herself that she could do no more. She didn't know what clothes Jacque would want to wear, and she wouldn't dare presume his style choices for the journey home.

Finally, at 2:40, she heard a noise at the door leading to the out of the doors. He would have to rush if they intended to truly leave that day. Moving from the bathroom towards the living area, she realized it was knocking on the door she heard.

Leaving the bedroom, she moved past the sofa beside the fireplace, moving towards the door that had a view of the ski lifts. She was startled to see the red and blue lights in the distance flashing in an alternating sequence. Now moving at a hurried pace, she stopped in the middle of the living room when she saw a man in Ski Patrol gear standing on the other side of the glass door. Opening the door, she was quickly greeted by the officer, "Ete-vous la femme de Jacque de Leon?" His French spoken through his German accent made it difficult for her to comprehend. Taking a moment to decipher his question, she finally confirmed she was Madame de Leon. The officer quickly noted her American intonation; he shifted to speaking English; he told her to grab her coat and bag.

Entering the hospital, she did her best not to think the worst thoughts; she needed to send good thoughts to Jacque. Escorted to a waiting room, she listened intently while the officer from the ski patrol told the nurse who she was. Her limited knowledge of the German language left her struggling to understand them. What little she made out was the man confirmed she was Jacque's wife.

The nurse moved from behind the desk she was working at to sit beside Lee. Speaking in perfect English, she began by asking Lee if she preferred English or French to communicate.

"Either one," she said. The caregiver took that as a clue to converse in English. "We need you to fill out some forms on your husband's behalf. I am sorry to tell you I don't have much information for you at this time. Your husband was severely injured about halfway down the run; it took quite a bit of time to get him down the hill to the ambulance."

"So he is alive?" Lee questioned the nurse. Needing answers, she found herself growing angry at the insensitive nature of this person asking her to fill out forms.

"All I can tell you is that he still had a pulse when they took him from the ambulance." The nurse's response felt cold and uncaring.

Lee took the stack of papers from the women, all dressed in white, and began filling out the details. Sitting there, doing her best not to lose control, she peripherally observed a man sit down across from her. When she heard Gabriel's voice, she looked up to see no one was visibly there. Lee immediately laid the pen and incomplete documents down; she knew, without a doubt, her husband was dead.

Lee's return to reality occurred when a surgeon entered the waiting room. Introducing himself, he asked if she would like to see her husband. She was aghast at the question being asked. Realizing it was an assumption that he was dead, she looked up to the surgeon and began to rise. Of course, she wanted to see her husband; what stupidity was this?

Guiding her down the corridor toward a room, the doctor explained they had done all they could to save him. "Currently, he is paralyzed from the waist down. The amount of blood he has lost is significant; the next forty-eight hours will determine his fate. I will leave you with him for a few minutes, and then he will need to rest."

"I guess I should have stayed in bed with you," Jacque wearily said. His eyes barely open, the bruises on his face forcing them to close. "Will you forgive me for this?"

She whispered to him while stroking his hand. "My love, it's not your fault."

"There's a man over there; he says I can go with him."

"Don't leave me. I will take care of you no matter what!" Lee shouted at Jacque through her tears, commanding him to rail against death.

As she watched her husband's stare go blank, she felt her father's touch on her shoulder.

CHAPTER 11

A small sliver of light fell across Lee's face interrupting her much-needed sleep. Giving in to the light piercing her eyelid, she allowed herself to give into morning's call. Realizing she was in the bed at the ski lodge, she began to shake as the events from the day before came into her head. Looking over to Jacque's side of the bed, she began to calm down as it was disheveled; she also heard humming in the bathroom shower. Working through the grogginess consuming her being, she interpreted the events so fresh in her memory must have been a nightmare. Pushing herself to find a state of calm and become fully aware of her surroundings, she rose from the bed and reached for her robe. It was not where she usually laid it. Looking around the room for where she had left it, she caught a glimpse of herself in a mirror. Seeing the clothes she wore when the paramedics arrived still on her body, she returned to panicking. Entering the bathroom to discern who was in the shower, she began to cry upon seeing Tino wrapping himself in a towel as he exited the tiled enclosure.

The feeling of Gabriel touching her shoulder as Jacque died left Lee unconscious. She had no recollection of events from that moment until now. Lee cried out, "What are you doing here? What day is it?" She felt herself going mad, rambling loudly while trying to make sense of things.

"You called the family the day before yesterday, telling them Jacque was gone and that you needed to find me. I left Madrid and headed here on the next plane. I came as quick as I could." Tino continued with the details of his arrival and of her retrieval from the hospital. "They admitted and kept you under sedation until I arrived. I had to lie and tell them I was your brother; thank God you had that picture of us in Paris in your wallet. The admissions nurse was the saving grace; she said she recognized me from the photo in your purse. When I confirmed the details of where the picture had been taken, they took my calling card and didn't ask any more questions."

Feeling her knees giving way, Lee leaned back against the wall and slid down to the tile floor. Pulling her legs up to her chest, she began to cry, "What am I going to do now?" Tino crossed the room and slid down the wall next to her. "First, we are going to get you back to Paris. Arrangements have to be made for his memorial." For the first time, Tino was serving a purpose that was not self-indulgent. Lee was somewhat surprised by his take-charge manner. She was thankful he was there.

Returning to Paris, Lee was numb inside while walking through the rituals of burying her husband. Jacque had his affairs in good order, and there was not much to decide beyond the choice of flowers and what to serve for dinner after the memorial. Lee was grateful her late husband had laid everything out so neatly. They had never discussed his choice of cremation and internment at the family crypt; this was news to her and gave her a deeper appreciation for how well Jacque had taken care of her.

Jacque's mother pushed back at the idea of cremation for her child. Tino quickly intervened and politely but firmly reminded Madame de Leon it was her son's wish. Tino was a stronghold for Lee, and she realized she would not have been able to manage the process without him by her side.

Those in the Laverde family who were able to attend the services arrived the morning of the memorial, staying on afterward to help Lee in any way they could. Her cousin and Tino appeared to be inseparable, and Lee wondered if death had given them a cause to reconcile.

The five-bedroom apartment felt empty to Lee; even though every bedroom was occupied by a family member, she felt alone. She did not know how she would cope with the loss of her husband. Even when Lydia passed, she had not felt this level of heartbreak. She recalled her reaction when Gabriel died; it seemed that each person she lost had a more significant emotional impact on her than the one before. Perhaps this was a part of her learning to love while overcoming her abandonment issues. And yet, here she was, once again, all alone.

For the year it took to settle Jacque's estate, Lee did not participate in life; she assigned the tasks to Tino. This allowed her solace to grieve the loss of her husband and the child they never conceived; the time also allowed Tino to prove he was now capable of managing conflict head-on as well as earning his keep. It was a win-win for each of them.

The de Leon family was very kind to her and gracious on most fronts. She assured them the money Gabriel had left her, along with her own assets, were defined in the pre-nuptial agreement. Lee received what money Jacque had in his personal accounts, along with his personal effects. Gifts, mementos, and items they had collected during their time together. The only argument to occur was about the apartment where they resided. The penthouse on the eighth floor, with a view of the Tour d'Eiffel, had been in his family for over sixty years. The de Leon's had no intention of allowing Lee to keep it.

Tino solidified his place in Lee's life when he resolved the challenge without the expense of an attorney. His ability to gather information that people chose to keep private was an easy task for him, after all. Providing Lee with the necessary information, Lee met with Madame de Leon over lunch to discuss a buyout of the property. The tilting point in the conversation came when Lee asked her mother-in-law a simple question. "Did your mother spend any time in jail after pushing your father over the balcony railing?" Without any further comment made, Jacque's mother quickly agreed to sign over the property.

Tino had gathered the information surrounding the man's mysterious fall to the street below. The events leading to this event in 1969 was a family secret that needed to remain buried alongside the man. Lee's mother-in-law was shocked that Jacque's wife would stoop to blackmail. She was even more surprised the young girl knew the story; even Jacque was not aware of the circumstances surrounding his grandfather's death. Madame de Leon did not know how Lee found out but was not willing to risk any other past events to rear their ugly heads. The de Leon's wealth had grown year over year and not always by legal means.

With her husband's family removed from her life completely, Lee honestly did not know what to do. She felt as if the little girl from the backwoods of Texas no longer had a purpose. The Laverde clan called on occasion but rarely visited. She didn't know why this bothered her so, but it did. They had been so welcoming to her when she arrived, Ernesto and Tino taking her under their wings, hosting her wedding. Had it not been for them, she would have never been exposed to all the things she needed to learn.

Placing her hand gently around the demi-tasse sitting on the wrought iron table, she rose from her perch and made her way to the edge of the terrace on the eighth floor. Peering over the edge, she wondered what Jacques' grandfather thought as he plummeted the eighty feet to his death. Perhaps she should find out and join her husband and father in the afterlife. Tino passed through the terrace doors just as he heard the screaming from the street below.

Rushing to the terrace edge, he looked down to see people screaming up at Lee. Her porcelain cup had shattered completely when it hit the cobblestone walkway below, splattering its contents and shards of clay on the cars and pedestrians below her. Fortunately, no one was hurt, including herself.

Lee agreed to enter an asylum for mental health after tossing her cup over the balcony's edge that morning. Tino knew the look in her eyes; he saw it in his mother's just before she shot herself in the head. It's a look an eight-year-old never forgets.

Driving Lee to the institute that very morning, Tino observed his friend check herself in. Initially, he was furious with her upon discovering he was not designated as her trustee or given power of attorney. That role was assigned to his former lover, her cousin. Calling the house in Madrid, Tino told the man he had once loved of the recent events and the need for him to be in

Paris immediately. It would be his duty to oversee the day-to-day activities of Lee's life.

Tino had run the house since Jacque died, even going as far as to write out the paper checks for any bills needing to be paid. Even though tempted, he never signed them or played hide and seek with her funds. He recalled all too well how she had forced his hand with the Laverde jewelry; he knew better than to trigger her intransigent nature she kept hidden. Now, feeling as if she still didn't trust him, Tino sought to remove himself from the demands of running her life. Handing all the files, invoices, bills, and blank checks to Ernesto upon his arrival at the apartment, Tino promptly exited, leaving his ex to figure out everything on his own.

Moving on to the clinic, shortly after his encounter with Tino, Ernesto was surprised at how well Lee looked. He didn't know what to expect; he had a mental image of her wasting away, possibly near death. She greeted him with a kiss on both cheeks. As they walked through the solarium towards the grounds of the facility, Lee offered him something to drink. Smiling at her, he whispered, "A latte would be nice."

Lee returned the smile, a genuine expression of warmth. She knew he was chiding her and realized it was well deserved. "Just don't drop it; it's not that far to the ground." She continued looking into his eyes to see his reaction to her statement. It took a moment before Ernesto realized this was a healthy retort, a response from a woman who was attempting to regain her sense and her soul.

Arriving at a bench with a serene view of a nearby pond, they began to converse over matters of the heart and what the future might bring. Lee explained the initial counseling was helping her deal with her grief, and she now acknowledged locking herself away in pity was the wrong thing to do.

If her progress continued, her goal was to stay four additional weeks before returning to society. She asked Ernesto if it was reasonable for him to manage the house for that period of time. He willingly agreed to stay on, provided Tino was somewhere else. "I've never gotten over what he did and don't want to be around him. I thought we might reconcile at the funeral, but it didn't take long for me to be reminded of who he really was. He isn't a bad person per se, but I won't ever be able to trust him again."

Lee didn't ask any questions; she was learning to let others work their issues out on their own terms without input from her. She had never perceived herself as a control freak, but with the recent events, she was becoming aware of a different person within, someone she wanted to become. After Ernesto shared his concerns, she assured him she would request Tino stay away from the apartment from that point forward.

The rest of their visit that day was spent discussing family. Lee was happy to hear the goings on in Madrid and that everyone was in good health. A nurse summoned Lee for her afternoon appointment with her therapist, bringing their time together to an end. Escorting her visitor to the lobby, she bid him goodbye and walked down the marble hallway to her appointment. Turning back to the healthcare worker, Ernesto asked the young man to show him to the front door.

Accompanying him to the front of the building, the nurse turned to Ernesto and asked if he could speak freely. Ernesto nodded yes. "Your friend appears to be settling in very nicely." Smiling at the handsome man, Ernesto's eyebrows raised, waiting for the question to be made. "Is Tino her lover or just a friend?" Ernesto knew where this was going. Accessing his evil side, he responded. "Oh yea, they have been fucking for years! That's why he is on her payroll." The young man's face revealed his disappointment to find out Tino was off-limits to him. Saying goodbye, Ernesto smiled to himself all the way back to the apartment. He knew he had been cruel to the young man but also surmised he was doing the kid a favor by keeping him out of Tino's clutches. As Lee had requested, Tino didn't cross paths with his ex-lover for the remaining weeks Ernesto was in Paris.

Tino moved on past his irritation after a brief conversation with Lee on the subject of

Ernesto. Releasing his ego, he began to visit her every day. On her last day of treatment, Tino arrived in the Peugeot sedan to pick her up and return her to her home. Lee wasn't sure how she would react to entering the apartment containing so many memories of her dead husband, but she finally felt emotionally strong enough to move on with her life. Entering through the front door, most of the memories present were good ones. She and Jacque had never fought; the time spent here had all been good. She would learn to live alone in the home he provided for her.

A Chance Meeting

CHAPTER 12

After two weeks at home, Lee decided it was time for a getaway. Being alone in the apartment was impacting her healing process.

She gave Tino directions to book her on a transatlantic cruise to the US. She wanted to return to Texas to visit and wanted the trip to not be rushed; she also had a task for him while she was gone.

Gabriel's boating accident had never settled with her; she thought it odd. Through her therapy sessions, she recalled how he was acting differently the day she left for Madrid. She figured if anyone could find out if something was amiss, it was Tino. He was to go to Columbia and dig into what really happened to Gabriel while she visited the States.

Taking the TGV from Paris to London appeared to take less time than the car ride from St. Pancras station to the port in Southhampton. Walking the gangway onto the QE2, Lee was surprised at the grandeur and beauty of the boat. She was impressed with the attention to detail on the ship and how precise everything was. Her sense was this would be a trip she would never forget. Making her way to the suite Tino booked for her at the aft, she was struck by how large the ship was. Lee made a mental note to herself to ask someone how many people were aboard.

Initially somewhat put off by the size of her cabin, she quickly reminded herself the room was around the exact size of the house she grew up in; it would do quite nicely. With her recent visit to the asylum, she had been introduced to what the doctor referred to as Cognitive Therapy. The methodology served her well; whenever a negative feeling caught her attention, she would mentally stop and ask why. It was work that had to be done.

Her valet greeted her promptly upon her arrival at the cabin. Introducing himself, Arturo began to sort her bags. Noticing his accent, she asked if she might practice speaking Spanish with him. He was immediately endeared to the beautiful woman he would assist for the next seven days. As Lee began assessing her luggage, Arturo handed her the life vest hidden in the closet by the cabin door, explaining that she must attend the safety drill. "I will prepare your room during the drill, and when you return, everything will be in its place. Should anything not please you, tell me the concern, and it will be addressed."

Lee quietly stood at the back of her assigned muster station, leaning against the wall during the announcements and the consecutive horn blasts from the bridge. She was suddenly reminded of how different her coloring was from the white people surrounding her. Her cognitive therapy working overtime, she decided she would utilize French as her primary language during the crossing to New York. She was curious to see how she was perceived by these people; if they thought her use of the English language was limited, they would be more carefree with their spoken opinions.

A woman standing to her left unexpectedly handed Lee an empty champagne glass while requesting a refill. This act of snobbery sent Lee back in time; her newfound mental processing technique was flung into the ocean. The woman reacted in shock when Lee looked at her and said, "Mais, non!" Lee let the coupe fall towards the floor while pursing her lips at the "old white woman." Fortunately, a staff member observed the interaction, and his quick reaction saved the glass from shattering on the deck.

He offered an apology to Lee in French and then leaned into the woman and whispered into her ear. Her eyes widened, and she quickly apologized for her behavior. Lee did not hear what the man said but smiled to herself, sensing the woman had been put in her place by the crew member.

She assumed the four-karat marquee diamond on her ring finger would have suggested to the woman they were equals; she then determined that people of this woman's class paid no attention to anything beyond themselves.

The Atlantic crossing was smooth and without incident for the first six days. Lee enjoyed the days in the sun by the pool, relaxing while reading the latest novel from her favorite author, Danielle Parks. She found the food delightful and looked forward to the excuse to dress for dinner every evening. She had not worn much else beyond bed clothes and workout wear since Jacque had passed. Fortunately, her figure had improved as she ate very little during the past eighteen months.

She utilized the makeshift jogging track every morning and began to feel herself returning. Her table companions consisted mostly of widowed women, much older than she. Whether intentional or not, they were very helpful to her as each had been in Lee's shoes. They understood the challenges of learning to live again without a mate. A few were crude with their remarks, how they were grateful their husbands were gone. Lee's favorite remark, albeit in poor taste, was what a dowager from Surrey said, "It's a matter of life after death, my sweet. Now that he's dead, I have a life!" Most of her companions carried the same sadness Lee was encountering; this gave her hope there was, indeed, life after death.

On their last night on board the QE2, the "Merry Widows," as the group had named themselves, insisted Lee join them for cocktails in the piano bar. Lee avoided alcoholic beverages for the most part during the trip; drinking was not conducive to honing the skill of cognitive therapy. However, a proper vintage of champagne uncorked would undoubtedly sway her to participate.

Sitting with the group of women who had been so kind, she ordered a bottle of Krug Blanc de Blancs to share amongst them. The bottle appeared in its ice bucket almost instantaneously. The first pour was tested by Lee to ensure it was acceptable. With a nod to proceed, the coupes were filled and served to each of the women. She closely watched their faces for expressions of appreciation; she wanted to know who understood excellence. Lee giggled at the pace the liquid was consumed. Most of the women were excited to enjoy champagne without a catch attached to the bottle's opening! When another bottle was ordered by a party member, Lee spoke to the server in French, suggesting he tell the woman the price.

"I will be happy to retrieve that for you, madame. Please confirm for me, $300 per bottle is acceptable." The women all stopped and looked first at the server and then at Lee, "I am aware of the price. I know the family who owns the vineyard."

Lee had learned early on never to discuss money or mention the cost of something unless necessary. She feared the woman could not afford it based on discussions had during their dinners. She felt she was protecting the woman, but her efforts landed differently than intended.

The situation becoming awkward, Lee began to make her excuses to leave the group. Saying her goodbyes, Lee began her exit. As she moved from the seating area towards the stairwell, a woman from behind her touched her shoulder. Lee slowly turned to see who was touching her. A sense memory had been triggered, she knew the smell of this person, and even though she couldn't place it, she needed to see this person face forward.

"I hope I didn't startle you, but I overheard you say you knew the family who owned Krug

Blanc. I am looking for a unique place for an executive meeting for my team. Any site producing sellable goods is always a hit. I know it presumptuous on my part, but I hoped you might be able to introduce me to the family of the vineyard."

The timbre of her voice, the sense memory of her pheromones, and the familiar nose, Lee recognized the woman approximately fifteen years her senior. As she introduced herself, it was obvious to Lee; the woman did not know who she was."Forgive my manners. I'm Blanch, Blanch Murrel."

CHAPTER 13

Waking up that morning, Blanch knew something was wrong. Standing up from the edge of the bed, she found herself wobbling before falling to the floor. Now over forty, she knew to not be surprised by unexpected bodily events. Frequently, pops and creaks would occur when simply raising from a chair or rotating her wrist. It was part of the aging process, or so she had been told. After the dizziness stopped, she gingerly lifted herself into the chair near her bed. She assumed it was low blood pressure or blood sugar. After sitting in the chair for a few minutes, she attempted to stand again and make her way to the bathroom. Had she not needed to urinate so badly, she would have remained in the chair a while longer. After relieving herself, she made her way back to the chair and reached for the phone. She was becoming concerned as the dizziness had returned after her visit to the toilet.

Bobby did not answer his phone when she rang him that morning, a major source of irritation for Blanch. Bobby was well aware he must be available whenever his boss called, and Blanch did not care that it was 1:30 AM in Dallas; she needed her assistant now. Redialing the number again, her aggravation grew as the ringing on the other end of the phone continued. Annoyed, she slammed the phone down. She had meetings scheduled and was not in the mood to be inconvenienced by health matters or an assistant's ineptitude.

Attempting to prepare herself for her first client of the day, she did her best to bathe and dress. Walking into the dining room in the hotel she was staying at; she spotted her customer across the room. Gently waving to him, she proceeded to make her way towards the two-top where he was seated. Using every table as a handrail for her journey, she apologized to the people she bumped into while crossing the room. Arriving at the table, she fell into the chair across from her breakfast guest.

Steven Dell looked at Blanch and immediately began a medical assessment. Having served as a GP prior to joining his uncle's company, he knew something was terribly wrong with the woman he was meeting that morning. "I appreciate your attempt to keep our appointment, but I think it is appropriate that we get you to hospital." Steven rose from the table and made his way to the hostess stand. Returning to Blanch, he informed her an ambulance was on its way. Asking if there was anyone he should notify, Blanch spouted out the home and work numbers for her assistant.

Waking from his sleep to the telephone ringing, Bobby was annoyed more than ever at his boss's intrusion. He had only been in bed for two hours and asleep for thirty minutes at best when the phone began to ring. He quickly grabbed the phone to avoid waking his sleepover guest. Answering it abruptly while muttering how rude he thought she was to be calling at the late hour. Mustering up the professional politeness utilized by his demanding boss, he gingerly said good morning into the receiver. He was not expecting a proper English accent on the other end of the line.

His tone quickly changed as he received the information of Blanch's arrival at the local hospital. Reaching for pen and paper, he jotted down the name of the facility she was being admitted to. Steven apologized to Bobby for not knowing the phone number but assured him it was the only hospital in Kensington.

Blanch did not like being the center of attention, especially in situations she was not in control of. Arriving at the hospital, gaining admission was a series of challenges as she was not a British citizen. As soon as they determined she was not in critical condition, services ceased until they knew whether or not she could pay the fees for her visit. An eternity passed for Blanch while she waited on someone to answer her questions and free her from the IV stuck in her forearm. When a nurse finally entered the room, she smiled at Blanch. Speaking with a strong cockney accent, Blanch could barely understand what she was saying. "We have had a phone call from your assistant in the US; he has provided all the information necessary. It'll be at least another hour before a doctor will be available." Sticking a needle into the IV port, the nurse squeezed the syringe emptying its contents into the saline solution. "This will calm you down, love, and let you rest until she can see you." Blanch did not like being given drugs by strangers in a place where she didn't know anyone. Her concerns did not last long; she was quickly asleep from the sedative.

Waking up from a lengthy snooze, she found the small treatment area where she had been placed upon arrival empty. Reaching for the call button, she knocked a small plastic box to the floor. The sound of the box's contents scattering across the floor caught the attention of a woman on the opposite side of the curtain that separated the beds. The unattractive striped linens slid back unexpectedly; the woman peering through the opening smiled and informed Blanch she would be with her in just a moment.

After completing the examination, Dr. Purohit said, "It appears you have a serious inner ear infection which is why you are dizzy. We will give you an antibiotic injection along with oral steroids. You should be good to go. How long are you planning to stay in London? You cannot get on a plane until the infection is gone, or you'll risk damaging your ear drums."

Blanch was not amused at the diagnosis and what it meant for her sales calls. She assumed Bobby did his job and canceled her afternoon appointment. There would be hell to pay if he hadn't. "When can I go back to my hotel room? I need to start arrangements to head back to the States." The physician smiled at her, "We can have you out of here in about an hour, I think."

Exiting the small, curtained area, the good doctor pulled the fabric closed behind her before shouting directions to the nurses. She spoke with such speed Blanch struggled to comprehend what was said.

Within the hour, Blanch received the medicine as prescribed and was in a taxi on her way back to her hotel. The driver had been given instructions to help her into the lobby. Appreciative of the extra level of service, Blanch tipped him quite generously for his assistance. Finally, in her room, she dialed the country code for the US and then the direct line to Bobby's desk.

Through his amazing efficiency and connections in the travel industry, Bobby managed to book Blanch on a boat back to New York. Blanch was not overly pleased with his plan until he explained that all the rooms at the hotel were reserved for the next ten days.

"I can find you another place if you prefer, but doesn't it make more sense for you to recover on the QE2 rather than be stuck in a London hotel." She was not thrilled with the option but agreed to be in South Hampton the following day to board the ocean liner.

The next three hours were spent with her dictating activities for her executive team. Bobby was to dispatch the directives to the staff. While out of touch for seven days, she did not want it to feel like a vacation for those at work in the Dallas facility. Bobby assured her he would follow up daily.

Finally resigning herself that she must leave the conversation and gather her belongings to pack, she told Bobby goodbye. There was no "Thank you" for the fantastic travel management or quick turnaround to get her back home, no apology for invading his time away from the office; this was a way of life for anyone who worked for Blanch Murrel. Bobby was the first assistant to survive her maniacal way of being for an extended period of time.

There were perks Bobby enjoyed; the badge he wore most proudly was that of being the assistant to one of the most powerful women in Dallas. He knew things, many things he should not have. Since her take over of Fergus, the company had grown exponentially, and Bobby was aware of every skeleton buried during her reign.

The boat was not what Blanch had expected. She appreciated its old-world elegance but thought it outdated and somewhat archaic. Blanch was used to having her way and getting what she wanted, and on this boat full of English society, Blanch did not carry any importance. Her request to sit by herself during dinner was only accomplished after an enormous cash tip was discreetly given to the Maître D' personally. Typically single travelers were grouped together; Blanch would not stand for that.

She was content to be on her own as usual, standing on the sidelines watching her life-mates perform their antics as if they were somehow important. This also allowed her to observe who might be of value to her or her company. Knowing only two more years remained until the equity investors in her company recouped their investments, she was always looking for new opportunities and people who could assist her in achieving her goal of being independent.

Blanch had been standing nearby Lee at the life jacket drill before departing South Hampton. She witnessed the woman assume the exotic dark girl was ship personnel, and she was impressed with how the young woman responded. Blanch noted the strength within the response to the older American woman; this young lady was a woman of means. Blanch would ensure they would meet before the ship arrived in New York.

There was something familiar to Blanch about Madame de Leon, but she couldn't place her finger on it; it was a distant sense she could not identify. Observing her with the group she engaged with, Blanch sat near their group to eavesdrop on their conversation on more than one occasion. The expensive bottle of champagne served to her friends on the last night of their voyage provided the opportunity Blanch needed to meet her.

Lee was kind to Blanch; she never blinked an eye or shifted her speech from the lovely French accent. It would have been easy for her to slip into that familiar East Texas accent when hearing Blanch speak; she did not want anyone on the boat to learn any more about her than they already knew.

Through the tragedies of her life, especially losing Jacque, Lee learned to control her outward emotions and hide her feelings. Seeing Blanch again after all these years, the sound of her voice, along with the familiar smell, removed the years that had passed. This was difficult for her; she was mentally back on the porch of that house in Palestine, Texas. She could hear Lydia and Blanch with raised voices arguing as they often did when she was a toddler. Lee lost in her mind for a moment, flinched slightly when Blanch touched her arm. Collecting herself in the present, she smiled as Blanch reached out her hand.

"Here's my business card; I would appreciate your sending me the contact information for your friends at the Krug factory. If you are ever in Dallas, let's have dinner and drinks."

Lee pondered for a moment whether she should continue engaging Blanch or move on and forget her. After all that had happened, the sadness she felt left her wondering if she would be better served to simply walk away.

"Perhaps when I am there, I will look you up. I have business there with some old acquaintances in the near future." Lee wondered if, by chance, her dear trustee would know what Blanch was up to these days; she would be sure to ask Garret after she arrived in Texas the following week.

Growing weary of dealing with the woman who didn't want her as a child, Lee excused herself and left without further acknowledging Blanch. Quickly making her way to her suite, she began to tremble upon opening its door. Entering the cabin, she immediately moved to her bedroom, where she hoped no one would notice the howling about to erupt from within her.

Forgetting this night was the final one on the voyage across the Atlantic, she sat on the floor and cried until a knock on the suite's front door occurred. Lee was soon confronted by her valet, who had arrived to prepare her personal effects for departure the following day. Unable to hide her tear-stained face, the service provider apologized and began to back out of the room. "I will come back after a while, Madame." Lee stood up from her crouched position on the floor, suggesting a moment of privacy to change out of her evening gown before they began to pack. A simple nod confirmed he would wait by the door while she attempted to pull herself together.

Returning from the bathroom in a pair of jeans and a simple pullover sweater, she moved from the bedroom to the salon but was not able to find the valet. Finally, it dawned on her that he must be waiting in the hallway, which of course, was the appropriate thing to do. Pulling the door open, she invited him back into the room. Propping the door open, he removed her trunk from its storage place and prepared it for her belongings.

Lee was grateful for the help that evening; it forced her to focus on something other than Blanch Murrel. A diversion she desperately needed. When she lay down to sleep, the memories of her past quickly filled her dreams. Thankfully the fitful night of rest was short-lived due to the early arrival in New York Harbor.

Her elite status on the ship allowed her to exit the liner later than most passengers. She hoped her car would be waiting for her with her luggage already loaded. The intent was to avoid any opportunity to see her long-lost birth mother.

Her driver was waiting for her just beyond the customs agents' desks. As soon as she finished with immigration, the driver would sweep her away. The port authority agent thoroughly reviewed every page of her passport. Asking the standard questions while peering up from the little blue book randomly, the government official made sure to stare her in the eye. Lee's responses were quiet and concise in English, using her Texas accent for the agent; she didn't want any reason to delay her journey.

Crawling into the back seat of the Mercedes limousine, she heard Blanch calling out after her. Pretending she didn't hear, she pulled the door closed while telling the driver to hurry up and pull away. As the car moved away from the curb and into traffic, Lee saw Blanch arrive at the edge of the car door out of her periphery. Pretending to be reading a document, she ignored her. Lee, still struggling internally, did not want to deal with Blanch and doubted she ever would.

Arriving in Dallas at the regional airport, Lee was greeted by Garret at the head of the gangway. She didn't realize it was him at first, as she had not laid eyes on him since she left Texas. "Bonsoir, madame. Comment çava?" Lee was impressed with how well he spoke French. "I am well but quite tired. The sailing wasn't as smooth as I had hoped it would be."

Sensing Lee was not in her best place emotionally and fully aware of her suicidal thoughts after Jacque's death; he offered to collect her luggage and take her to her hotel immediately.

There was much to discuss regarding her trust and investments, but they had a week to accomplish what was needed. No reason to dive in straight away. In the car on their way to the Mansion on Turtle Creek, no words were spoken. The passengers both sat quietly in the back seat of the limousine, observing the streets of Dallas.

Pulling into the hotel courtyard, Lee reached for his hand before speaking. "She was on the boat. That fucking cunt was on the same goddamned boat!"

CHAPTER 14

Sitting in the boardroom across from the men who managed her funds, Lee remained silent while they reviewed her estate. Hidden behind their veil of concern, they were desperately seeking information regarding monies left by her dead husband. Following the lessons learned from the Laverde's, she used silence to respond; she kept the life she developed in Europe out of the conversation with these men. Not being a fool by any means, she was aware of their greed and the hopes of holding her euros in their international coffers and therefore earning the interest. Lee also knew that each of these men, except Garret, wanted to bed her. She was rich, sexy, incredibly fit, and dressed in such a manner each of these attributes was voiced.

One of the things she appreciated about the European mindset was the fact that one could remain feminine while showing strength. Lee had never developed an appreciation of the American model for women, where exhibiting feminine traits was perceived as a cry out for a man to render aid.

Listening to each of their assessments, she arrived at a conclusion. She needed to invest in something that would generate a better return on the cash she had. Her current investments generated enough income to pay her advisors commissions and nothing more. Many suggestions were made about where to utilize the funds, but she didn't like any of them. She didn't want a clothing line; she liked her personal style and didn't want to replicate it for others. She wasn't a designer, and even with her impeccable sense of style, she feared the stresses of styling clothes would overwhelm her and remove her joy of fashion. One suggestion was made that she should use her connections in Europe and start an import/export business. Proposal after proposal was made; none of them successfully.

Returning to the Mansion and arriving in her room, she made her way to the marbled bathroom to remove the grime of Dallas from her skin. It was then she recalled what the man in St.

Moritz said. That was the answer; she would start her own skincare line.

When she awoke early the following morning, the first thing she did was cancel her appointments for that day. Making her way to a nearby shopping center, she spent hours on end researching skincare offerings in the department stores.

As she had previously encountered, color pigments for dark-skinned women were difficult to find in the United States. Even after the recent U.S.-driven "Black is Beautiful" campaign, companies ignored the need for dark pigment skincare for women of color. This was the driving factor why she never wore foundation. Her search at the makeup counters in the high-end stores revealed most sales clerks had no education in dealing with darker skin tones. These two things combined convinced her this was the best way to invest her money.

Returning to her advisors the following day, she told them her wish and suggested they start their due diligence to ensure her idea would be profitable. Lee felt a spark in her she had not known since before Jacque died. It was a sense of purpose, and she needed to feel she had a reason for living. "I am leaving for Paris tomorrow on the Concorde; I will return to Dallas in three weeks to hear your suggestions. Will that be enough time to prepare a proposal?"

Seeing the shift in Lee's demeanor, the men in the room agreed to have recommendations available to her by the time she returned. Wrapping up the meeting, she announced to her team that she would not combine her assets. "I am willing to invest everything being overseen by this team into this venture. I believe in this project wholeheartedly and sense it will give me purpose and help many other women who look like me. The assets acquired from my deceased husband will remain where they are. I am sure you understand the logic in this move." Garret was beaming with pride as if his child had taken her first steps.

Before boarding her plane, she made a short but concise call to Tino requesting he access his European contacts who had knowledge of the skincare industry. She wanted him to arrange meetings with them for her. She knew it was imperative she increase her level of knowledge, as well as understand who the players were; after all, these companies would be her competition. Lee also wanted an update on what Tino had discovered on his journey to South America.

Her business plan to develop and capture her target audience of women who weren't white was a secret she kept to herself. She would disclose this information on a need-to-know basis. Lee knew this critical bit of information was the key to her success. Several of the larger companies in the industry were attempting to reel in the dark-complexioned consumer. Still, they didn't understand the market, and leadership by dark-skinned women did not exist in the skincare world, at least until now.

Tino met Lee in Dallas when she returned three weeks later. Meeting with her financial advisors on her new adventure, the duo was impressed with the amount of detail presented in the research. Details focused on profitability and chances of success but severely lacked demographic information. She was discouraged by how the numbers given to her by the supposedly knowledgeable support team implied her dream was not likely a successful venture. She again felt as if she was being put in her place and told to return to the kitchen.

Lee had been away from Texas long enough that she forgot how women were viewed and expected to follow a man's recommendation. Lee considered the possible damage she might cause to her project if she said what she was thinking; the possible repercussions did not dissuade her from speaking. "Gentlemen, I wonder if Mary Kay was sitting here if you would give her the same advice?" Her trustee knew precisely where Lee was headed with this statement. He quietly looked around the room, observing the men's faces as they realized they were about to receive a dressing down by the young woman at the head of the table. "The company formation process has already begun in France. I hoped your research would persuade me to start the company here in the States where I was born, but alas, you have failed to sway me."

Tino was surprised to see the power with which Lee delivered this message to the men in the room. He had not witnessed this level of passion in her in all the years since they had met. Something had triggered her; it excited him, but it also gave him pause. He recalled the incident in Madrid at the wedding; he remembered her tenacious side all too well. But this was different, more mature, more directed; he needed to make sure she never became cross with him again.

"Robert, you are the senior accountant, correct? I need you to combine my assets into one pool. I want readily available cash to access as I need it." Lee looked from one man to the other, making her way around the large wooden conference table; she made her presence known. As the men gazed into her eyes, they became increasingly aware Madame de Leon was no longer to be their cash cow. Retrieving their charts and handouts, the men rose from their seats and exited the room. Each of them had other clients' assets to manage, but hers had been their primary focus as it was the easiest to earn their commissions.

Garret merely asked Lee if she was sure about her request, nothing more was said until Tino was asked to wait in the lobby. Tino exited the room leaving Lee and Garret to discuss the future. Lee laid out the information she had gathered about dark pigment skin and the unwillingness of the major cosmetics company to serve the market. "Most of the women who look like me are blending multiple products in order to get a color somewhat near their own. I learned of at least two women who approached major brands in an attempt to create products, but they were turned away. There is a golden ticket right here in front of us."

Garret trusted Lee's insight and confirmed he would follow up with the change to her fund as requested. "Do you have a plan for where you want to manufacture the products?" Garret was digging for information, and Lee knew it. He knew of the company Blanch had taken over and was aware of how small the skincare manufacturing world was; he didn't want Lee to be caught off guard should she and Blanch cross paths again.

"As I mentioned in the car in front of the hotel, I met Blanch Murrel on the boat from England. I am aware of her business here in Dallas."

Garret sat very still, he couldn't read the woman across from him, and he didn't want to be the trigger releasing her anger. "After what you called her in the car that afternoon......" Lee interrupted him.

"She was nice enough. She didn't have a clue who I was, and I made sure it stayed that way. What is it that concerns you, Garret? I assume you knew where and what she was up to these days." Lee stopped speaking and stared at her faithful trustee.

"I didn't want you to run into her and be surprised, but apparently, fate didn't agree with me on this. Our all too few correspondences through the years left me believing you were happy and had moved on from the past. I wasn't going to bring her up unless you asked. I hope you know I have done my best to protect you as much as possible." Garret smiled at Lee; it was then she noticed the slight bruise on his neck. She had not really observed him since she returned to Texas; she realized it was time to shift her focus from Blanch to him.

"Let's leave all that aside for now. How are things with you? Personally, I mean." Lee waited for his response without any emotion on her face. She did not want him to feel uncomfortable for any reason. Tino had kept her up to date with the news of the new gay disease spreading across New York and San Francisco. After spending time with Ernesto and Tino, she assumed Garret was gay. Lee assumed her openness about Tino's lifestyle allowed Garret to let his guard down a bit. Using his fingertips to lift the collar of his shirt up, he attempted to cover the purple lesion. After a few moments of silence in the room, Lee spoke. "Who knows? Have you told your wife?"

"Tessa doesn't know. At this point, only my doctors do. When she discovered I was sleeping with her best friend's husband, we parted ways. We are in the process of divorcing, and she will get everything. Doing it this way avoids so many issues, as my prognosis is not good. Six months at best."

Lee excused herself from the room to find Tino. Giving him a list of tasks to be completed, she told him to take the car and go; she would meet him back at the hotel later. "You are on your own this evening." With that said, she returned to the table and chairs where she had left her friend. He had not moved a muscle in her absence.

Garret had taken such good care of her over the years; the least she could do was to find out what she could do to help him. "Let's have some dinner this evening. Is there any new and hip place I need to know about?" Smiling at him, she reached for his hand and held it while he sobbed.

Pulling himself together, he rose from his seat and crossed to exit the room. "I will be back in ten minutes and will have made reservations somewhere exquisite." The physical shift in his stance improved as soon as he exited the door. This told Lee all she needed to know. Except for the men he slept with, no one beyond his wife and doctors had a clue he was a practicing homosexual. She felt a feeling of deep sorrow for him. It wasn't exactly empathy, but she understood the pain of being ostracized for being outside the allowed social deviance curve. She couldn't hide her unique qualities as they were visible, whereas he could transform himself to fit the mold as situations dictated. She didn't know which was worse, overcoming the color of her skin or his having to hide who he loved.

Both of them did their best to have the evening be as light-hearted as possible. It was several cocktails in before the hard questions started. How long had he known he was sick? What were his long-term plans, aka, was he planning to commit suicide? What had led up to the meeting with her mother? Answers to each of their questions prompted another, and so on the evening went. When Lee asked how Blanch had managed to own a company, Garret was not hesitant to share the specifics surrounding how she forced the owners out.

Lee was shocked to hear the intimate details he knew. "Not only was I the attorney for the family that owned the company, but I was also sleeping with her assistant. I didn't know Bobby worked for her until the information I thought I was sharing in confidence came back to bite me in the ass, and not in the fun way. Ah, good times." Garret smiled, thinking about the experiences he had enjoyed with Blanch's assistant prior to the betrayal. He momentarily wondered if Bobby was still with her.

Garret drove Lee back to the hotel on Turtle Creek; it was on the way to his small bungalow in Oak Lawn. Dropping her off, he felt better than he had in days. Perhaps it was the liquor mixing with his meds, or maybe it was that he knew he had at least one person in the world who accepted him for who he really was.

Riding the elevator to the penthouse, Lee made a promise to herself to have Tino find out if there was any treatment available in France that might be of help to Garret. Pondering how to ask without outing her friend, she entered the suite to find Tino on the couch waiting for her. Laying her clutch on the side table in the hallway, Lee crossed the room and joined him on the sofa. Inquiring about his evening, she gently inserted her request for knowledge into the conversation. Tino looked over at her and asked, "How long is he expected to live?" Lee was surprised he had picked up on the situation. Seeing the surprised look on her face, he laughed. "It's called gaydar; all gay men have it. It's how we find each other, and I saw the sarcoma on his neck." He promised Lee he would find out anything he could to see if they could help her friend.

Sleep was restless for Lee that night. Each time she woke, it was from a dream of Blanch. She couldn't decide if she was concerned more by the news of Garret's illness or what her mother had done to steal a business. Lydia did her best to raise her children to be better than that; she didn't understand. After a night of little sleep, she decided to take her mother up on the offer to connect.

CHAPTER 15

Tino didn't understand the nervous energy emitting from Lee that morning. She had been so strong in the room full of men just days before; he wondered what the root cause was generating the considerable angst in her.

Tino took the lead as they entered the large double glass doors leading into the corporate offices of Murrel International, the parent company of Fergus Manufacturing. Informing the receptionist they had a meeting scheduled with Blanch Murrel, Tino handed the woman manning the desk his card. With a simple smile, she pointed to the lobby while politely suggesting they have a seat; she would inform the team of their arrival.

Lee quietly observed the room; it gave her cause to chuckle to herself. The furniture was expensive and somewhat opulent but completely lacked style and taste. Whoever had been paid to decorate the room had obviously never set foot out of Dallas. This set the tone of her mood, causing her to finally relax. Tino inquired as to what she was giggling about. Aware the young women behind the desk could hear them, she responded in French. "Ça sent l'argent neuf." The decor represented everything wrong about new money, the 'odor of new money' was a phrase she had learned from Jacque, and it was apropos for the environment they were seated in. Utilizing her newly learned therapy skills, she reminded herself she too was nouveau riche and determined her mother had not been afforded the knowledge she received from the Laverde family.

Bobby opened the glass partition separating the lobby from the offices and greeted his boss's guests. His posture immediately improved upon laying eyes on the handsome European man in the lobby. Lee observed the shift in body language and thought to herself, "Gaydar." She was happy to have this unexpected engagement of male egos; it would serve useful if she chose to proceed with her plans.

"I am Ms. Murrel's assistant. Here is my card; feel free to call me if there is anything I can do to be of assistance or service." Seeing the name on the card, she became slightly giddy as she recalled what Garret said about Blanch's assistant, who liked to share information after a roll in the hay. Tino smiled politely at Bobby while quickly dismissing the portly assistant. Bobby was not the kind of man he was used to enjoying the company of; beefy boys were not his cup of tea. His playmates needed to be fit and have lots of stamina, just like him. Passing Bobby and moving into the tacky green and beige wallpapered conference room, Tino stopped when he heard Lee playing nice with Bobby. He was even more shocked by the heavy French accent spewing from her mouth. She had not told Tino about the incident on the boat and her need to present herself as a French aristocrat.

As Lee chatted with Bobby, a middle-aged man entered the room, followed by two other people. Each of them introduced themselves along with their respective titles; business development director, senior quality control specialist, and junior member of the R&D staff. After each of them completed their well-rehearsed micro speeches defining their responsibilities, Tino introduced himself with no implication of his title or purpose. Then he introduced Lee as the owner of the French Company, Le Peau Sombre.

Refreshments were offered to Tino and Lee prior to the business development manager beginning his presentation. He, along with a quality control team member, shared basic information about the small company. The small talk occupied several minutes of the meeting while beverages were served. For effect, Lee would occasionally speak to Tino in French; she had begun to question why she was there.

Knowing the sales pitch drill so well, Bobby lowered the projection screen for the formal presentation right on cue. The slides were a succession of carefully laid out details of the long-standing manufacturing company and its purchase by Blanch. All the details of growth and value were charted in percentage points with only one reference to actual company value. The business development director answered the question on Lee's mind regarding the charts lacking monetary information. "We are privately held and do not share our financial information with potential customers. As a French company, I am sure you understand."

The statement from the company representative was perceived by Lee as a snub against the French way of doing business. She was fully aware most of the presentation was bullshit and was increasingly irritated her birth mother hadn't bothered to attend the meeting. Lee expressed her irritation to Tino in French; how dare the woman who invited her to meet hadn't bothered to offer up as much as a greeting. Observing the research staff member's reaction to her statement, she assessed the young woman must have understood what she said.

Before Lee returned to speaking English to the group, a note was passed to the team leader. Reading the message from his colleague, the director suggested they take a short break as something required his immediate attention. Making his apologies, he exited the room. Tino smiled at Lee before asking Bobby where the men's room was. Bobby offered to personally show him the way.

Lee sat at the table, looking through the glass partition overseeing the office filled with cubicles. The far side of the open-plan office ended abruptly against a wall with closed doors at the end of each walkway. The office doors sealed implied their inhabitants were not at the office or were removed from the low-level employees. Each entry was embellished with the name and title of its occupant. One office door ajar allowed Lee to see within; its decor of dark stained wood paneling and overstuffed Chesterfield-styled furnishings was off-putting to her. Observing everything she deemed wrong with this place, she momentarily thought about leaving and aborting her plan. Gabriel was right to send her off to see the world, its exposure gave her insight, and she once again realized how fortunate she had been. There was no need to open the door to a life where her birth mother was involved.

Tino and Bobby returned to the boardroom giggling like school girls; they had begun to bond.

Lee was glad; this meant she wouldn't have to ask Tino to whore himself out. As the team returned to the meeting, Blanch entered behind them with flair.

Her outfit, obviously expensive American couture, paled in comparison to Lee's daily wear. Lee was quick to perceive Blanch must be oblivious to such things. She greeted Tino and Lee and questioned if the team was taking good care of them. She was updated on where they were in the process of the meeting by the team leader. "I just shared with Lee our stance on our financials and non-disclosure as we are privately held."

Lee looked directly at Blanch before letting the smile on her lips fade. "I am sure you understand the size of this account will warrant a full audit of your capabilities which must include finance." Seeing the red on Blanch's neck creep upward, Lee was thrilled to see she had struck a nerve.

Attempting to control her verbal response, the reddish color rising up towards Blanch's cheeks did not align with the words coming from her lips. "Under a non-disclosure agreement, we should be able to accommodate the request. Provided we choose to work together." Blanch did not like being addressed so directly or overtly.

Typically sales meetings like this were left to the business development team, but in this instance, she had been summoned surreptitiously. Blanch was now in an awkward position; she had to save face in front of her employees and hopefully help sales win this account. Calming herself down, she asked Lee what the expected volume of orders would be during year one of sales.

Lee shared the long-term goal of the company at a very top level. She revealed she would be interviewing Research and Development teams in France and the United Kingdom. At the end of year one, she hoped to be prepared for initial manufacturing and planned to select her manufacturing partner within the next six months. Lee purposefully never answered Blanch's question regarding volume or expected revenue. She didn't have the data and had not hired the people necessary to provide the information. "This meeting is probably a little premature considering where we are in our development process, but since I was in Dallas and you invited me, it seemed appropriate."

Blanch sensed the opportunity was fading and quickly put on her game face to avoid losing this potential account. Then Lee said what Blanch wanted to hear, "I expect to invest, at a minimum, a million for development and advertising in the first year." This was a client Blanch wanted, someone who had the means and could salvage the financial mess she had created.

"Will you be seeking investors? We often partner financially with clients when it makes sense." The manufacturing team all looked at Blanch; they had never been privy to these types of arrangements. The reaction was noted by Lee before she responded. "Just as your team doesn't share its financial information, I won't be sharing ours. However, I will say the money driving this project is inherited family money." This was humorous to Lee; the money supporting this adventure was from Blanch's mother and grandparents.

After another hour of polite discussion, Tino and Lee exited the building. An invitation to dinner had been made by the sales team, but Lee declined. She simply stated it wasn't her way of doing business.

The team reluctantly returned to the conference room for a quick debrief of the meeting. Each of them had worked for Blanch long enough that they recognized the signs of her being in a foul mood. The magnet of the witch was not on the side of Bobby's desk, but they knew the drill.

After berating the team in a cleverly disguised, genteel soft tone, Blanch quietly asked each of them what had gone wrong. After the research team member shared that Madame de Leon had expected Blanch to personally handle the meeting, the owner's tone shifted. Blanch dismissed the team and returned to her office. After passing Bobby's desk, the warning sign magically appeared.

The pressures of running the company were building and would soon explode if she didn't find a profitable account. The years of "fixing" other manufacturers' issues had left the company bleeding financially. Blanch realized she was foolish to push out the investors, but she wanted total control and did not want to answer to anyone.

In her mind, she had driven the valuation of the company down before and rebuilt it, so why couldn't she do it again? The Director of Finance warned her a year ago that something had to change, or bankruptcy wouldn't be far off. She had a degree in finance, and she knew he was right, but her ego refused to let her believe it. On her way to rid the investors by devaluing the company, she knew she needed a solid win to get back on top of the game.

Bobby tapped on the door before entering her office, prepared to duck if a desktop item should come hurling towards him. "Is there anything you need before I leave for the day?" Bobby hated asking this question at the end of every day as there was always an excuse to keep him at the office past regular business hours. Should he forget to check in with her before he left, there would be a message waiting for him on his machine when he got home. Her response that day surprised him, a simple confirmation that nothing was needed.

Blanch was, simply put, irritated that the meeting had not gone as expected. She felt she always had a keen sense of people, that she could read them and intrinsically knew how to manipulate them. This woman was no different from most of the female businesspeople she met; they were hungry for power. Blanch sensed in her gut that Ms. de Leon had someone she wanted to get even with; she would have to work a little harder to find out who.

As was the norm, Bobby entered his apartment to the blinking light on his answering machine. He knew who it was before even pushing the play button. Listening to the message, he perked up hearing what his boss wanted him to do. A little espionage mission always excited him. Writing down the phone number to the posh hotel where Tino was staying, he wondered what these people had that Blanch wanted.

Making the call, he arranged a meeting time and place for drinks and possibly dinner with Tino. By the time he made the short drive to Oak Lawn, Tino was already at the Library Bar sipping a martini. Sitting down across from the handsome man, Bobby had visions of sugar plums dancing naked in his head.

Alone in her room, unaware of Tino's excursion to meet with Bobby, Lee revisited the day's events in her mind. She questioned if her motives in this game she had started were worth the energy. Coming to the realization that getting even with her birth mother was not in line with her mission, she talked herself out of seeking revenge. Lee wanted to establish a company that would honor all women; her desire to get even with Blanch had merely been a childish fancy. Back and forth she went: each time she talked herself out of the revenge model, she remembered how long and hard she cried when Blanch left home without saying goodbye. Had Blanch ever returned to the little house she grew up in, this would all be for not, but she never did. That was a thorn in Lee's side that even the strongest pair of tweezers lacked the strength to remove the barb inserted when she was a mere child.

Looking out over the Dallas skyline from the living area balcony, she heard Tino enter the hotel suite. She had been unaware he had left and now assumed he to be alone as she didn't hear anyone else with him. Closing the entry door, Tino waited a moment before making his way to the chair opposite her. "I didn't realize you had gone out, but I am glad you are back. Was it drinks and dinner or drinks and…" She knew how much Tino loved to explore a new man from head to toe, so she was slightly stunned when he responded, "Only drinks with Bobby."

Her gut reaction was to warn Tino about Bobby's past entanglement with Garret but felt it would be poorly received. Tino did not seem surprised nor reactive to the information Lee shared regarding Garret's past. He was surprised the handsome trustee found interest in the man he had met for drinks. Tino had been fortunate to remain negative in the early days when no one knew what was going on with the disease. He assured Lee he was safe in his sexual escapades. "Bobby has a lot of information in his head. He will be happy to tell me anything I want to know, but it will take some time to gain his trust."

Lee sat quietly for a moment, pondering the unexpected invitation from Bobby. She saw the two of them bonding at the meeting earlier that afternoon, but that had more of a girl's night out vibe. Granted, Tino was incredibly sexy. His perfect body, covered in expensive fabric caressing every curve of his muscles, allowed him the opportunity to bed just about anyone he sought. His looks were only outdone by his charisma; the combination of these two attributes made him very desirable. Even more so here in Texas. So why wouldn't Bobby chase after her friend? Still, something seemed out of the norm where this was concerned.

Lee muttered softly, "That will be useful when the time is right." Tino began his exit to the main living area; stopping at the sliding glass door, he turned back to face her. "I am not exactly sure what is going on with you. Are you sure you are OK? Your, how you say in English, 'comportement,' has changed. It's becoming dark." Lee was surprised Tino saw the shadows forming around her. "It's demeanor, the word in English, I mean. Lots on my mind, that's all. Don't forget I am going to see my hometown tomorrow."

Lee dreaded the drive to the town she left over a decade ago but felt she needed to see her life then and now. She also wanted to spend some time with her momma, Lydia. She and Tino were scheduled to return to Paris the day after; if she didn't make the trip to Palestine the next day, she didn't know when she would.

Going back to the no longer small town stirred many feelings she had not expected. There was a wave of anger forming in her, and she couldn't determine why. The only real negative she could recall, beyond the woman who raised her passing, was how Blanch had abandoned her.

The stone marking where Lydia's ashes had been scattered now sat in the middle of a city park. The land that was once used for farming was now covered in modern tract homes. Lee was surprised the small park had been established, thereby saving the burial grounds of her mother and her Nanna.

Sitting by the stone marking where Lydia Murrel's ashes had been spread, she contemplated what this overwhelming feeling was. She had long ago forgiven the people who mistreated her for being dark-skinned. Living overseas gave her insight into their ignorance, and she did not want to live a life filled with hate.

Time slipped away while she visited the grave; she had not realized the lateness of the afternoon until her escort cleared his throat behind her and suggested they head back to Dallas before dark. Lee kissed the marker and told Lydia she loved her and how sorry she was for staying away so long. Back in the rear seat of the car, she settled in for the long drive back to Dallas.

Sleep overtook her on the ride through the Piney Woods, and when she awoke, she noticed the feeling of Jacque nearby. She was glad for his presence while moving through the beautiful scenery of East Texas; it reminded her of their former home just outside Marseille. The comfort of his presence confirmed she was ready to go home to Paris. Lee hoped returning to the city, and focusing on her project, would shift her 'comportement' back to normal.

The three-and-a-half-hour flight to de Gaulle airport from DC took less time than the flight from Dallas to the capitol. Lee appreciated the speed and luxury of the supersonic jet; she preferred to not spend eleven hours on a plane, even if it was a direct flight.

Arriving back at the apartment, she was thrilled to be home but not overly excited to see the mail stacked up, begging for her attention. Tino usually sorted through everything and only passed on things to her that needed her review. She never worried about Tino hiding anything from her; important documents went straight to her personal PO Box. In addition, Garret had taught her at a very early age each and every document required two signatures to be transacted. She felt reasonably sure all was in order.

After a hot shower in her own space and donning a pair of silk pajamas, Lee poured herself a champagne cocktail and grabbed the stack of letters to sort through. Her posts were mainly invitations to events or solicitations she had no use for. Finishing her aperitif and the bottle of champagne re-corked, Lee placed the bottle in the chiller and moved to her bedroom. Finishing her evening ritual with her hair pulled into a braid, she slid into the sheets of her bed and was fast asleep.

CHAPTER 16

Looking back over the last few months, Lee was very pleased with the work accomplished by her and the team she was assembling. Seeking out the people she felt were best suited for the development of the business, she only hired those who showed a deep interest in the company's growth. She was amazed at how all the pieces came together, as if some outside source was working in her favor. The work kept her occupied, which helped to push her past the anger lingering in her soul after the visit to the US. The ongoing sense of loss she had for Jacque was felt every day; her work kept her focused and minimized the agony of being alone.

In addition to the sense of loss for Jacque, Lee received more disheartening news. Recently receiving a letter with a US Postal Stamp and no return address on the envelope, she was saddened by its contents.

Opening it, she was curious who it might be from as no one in Texas beyond Garret knew where she resided in France. The handwritten note was from Garret's ex-wife; he did not live as long as his doctors had predicted. Tessa explained the request found in his work papers that someone tell Lee of his passing. Included in the letter was Tessa's contact information.

Garret's wife suggested Lee reach out to her regarding her plans to work with Murrel Manufacturing. In her letter, Tessa explained the information found within Garret's ledger noted Lee's interest in Murrel International. She felt Lee would be interested to hear about Blanch's rise to glory. Lee didn't expect this woman she knew as a young girl to provide any information that would be pertinent, and she didn't trust the wives of Dallas to keep important info to themselves.

Saying a small prayer of thanks that Tino had not intercepted the letter, the contact information was filed away in Lee's personal safe. She would get in touch with Tessa in the future if there was a need. Lee wanted to maintain focus on building her team. The next major task for her was to find the right chemist to create her product line. Her intent for the next year was to focus on what she needed to accomplish and move away from the constant reminders of the past.

The preliminary business development consumed the bulk of the first year after Le Peau Sombre was officially founded. Developing its product line was foremost in Lee's mind; she gave no attention to Blanch's repeated attempts to connect. Being put off by the young entrepreneur, Blanch made a surprise visit to the offices of Le Peau Sombre. Lee did not interact with her birth mother for fear the dark cloud that surrounded her the last time she saw Blanch would return.

Tino gave Blanch a tour of the offices, excusing Lee from speaking with her; "She is busy in a meeting." Tino reported back that Blanch appeared desperate to talk with Lee. "Her tone and the questions posed made it clear she wanted to see only you!" He also shared his observation that all of Blanch's questions pointed to money. Lee thanked Tino for his insight, dismissed the thought, and moved on with her work.

By late spring, the groundwork had been laid; the product development was complete. Her skincare line was ready for marketing. Each product profile Lee set out had been achieved; she was thrilled her vision was being fulfilled. Safety testing was completed, and it was time to move from the laboratory to full-scale production.

With the money from her inheritance partially consumed, Lee was growing concerned funds would be depleted before the company would turn a profit. She despised the manner in which her industry counterparts had been treated by the large companies and opted to own the storefronts where the products would be sold; each location owned and operated by Le Peau Sombre. This was a substantial financial risk for a small start-up company.

Lee was not overly concerned with the threat. She spent a great deal of time carefully researching the fashion designers who were controlling their brands by limiting growth and exposure. The business model made sense to her; she was sure this was the best way to move her company forward.

Lee had fallen in love with the French methodology of work/home life balance. She insisted her employees have lives outside the organization and found employees were much more productive in the day-to-day. She also discovered her passion for her business overtook her emotions at times, leaving her friends' and companions' personal lives on the sideline. Cognizant of the behavior, her diary was kept clear every Thursday afternoon; she and Tino had a standing lunch date. This was an agreed-upon time away from work to discuss their personal lives. Tino had moved on from being Lee's, per se, boy toy; he was now a member of her management team. Earning his own money, he finally matured into a man she felt she could trust. He didn't like how she reviewed all his decisions but didn't take it personally, as Lee treated all her team members equally.

Sitting at a small table neatly tucked in a corner of a sidewalk cafe near the Seine, the two of them consumed chilled chardonnay. Tino had come to the conclusion it was time to broach the subject of Lee finding a new love. Jacque had been gone almost five years, and he felt it was time she enjoyed time away from work with a companion. Although Lee strove to keep a realistic balance between work and home, she had not succumbed to the French model of working to live. She was someone who lived to work. Bringing up the subject of Jacque, Tino noticed an immediate shift in Lee's mood. He wondered if he should quickly change the subject and avoid his friend's unhappiness, but before Lee could respond, a woman approached the table. Interrupting them, she asked for confirmation Lee was Madame de Leon. Looking up at the woman cautiously, Lee confirmed she was indeed her. Lee didn't recognize the woman but knew the unmistakable Texas accent and Dallas blonde hairstyle. Tino earned his keep once again by interrupting the woman and introducing himself. This ploy would force the woman to provide her name, hopefully giving Lee some insight into who their unexpected visitor was. "Hi there, nice to meet you. My name is Tessa Richards."

It was Garret's former wife, the girl from Lee's hometown in Texas. Lee was not sure how she had found her. "I apologize for the surprise, but I knew who you were from the promotional photos for your makeup line. Garret had copies of the teams' presentations to you in his files, and I have been following your work ever since. May I have a few moments of your time?"

Tino stood and offered his chair to Tessa, gave his love to Lee, and moved on to other activities. Lee graciously offered Tessa a glass of wine which she readily accepted. The conversation started off slowly, revolving around Tessa's previous visits to Paris. She spoke of her honeymoon with Garret in the city so many years before, her shopping sprees on the Champs Elysèes, and the usual tourist traps. Her tone when speaking of her dead husband gave Lee insight into the questions she needed answering. "There is no ill will towards Garret. I had figured out he was gay before he did, I think. We chose to divorce so we could live our lives authentically; we still loved each other and hated that we couldn't satisfy each other physically. When I found out he was sick, I tried to get him to reconcile, but he refused because he believed I would be better taken care of as a divorcée than a widow. Only a handful of people know what he actually died from and, with the exception of one person, had the decency to keep it to themselves. I don't know how she even found out."

Lee knew immediately who Tessa was talking about and knew firsthand exactly how Blanch found out Garret was dying. He made sure to tell Bobby he had been exposed to the virus; Garret wanted his former playmate to have every chance in the world to get ahead of the disease if he had contracted it. Lee wondered how long Bobby waited before telling his boss the news.

Tessa and Lee spent the rest of the afternoon discussing the future of Lee's emerging product line. Lee was surprised at how well-versed Tessa was in business dealings. Her comprehensive knowledge of operating a company gave Lee immense pleasure. Finally, to speak with another female who was not pushed into the background or played the doting wife.

Knowing many capable women who had the potential to do great things, it always saddened her to see them pushed aside due to their gender. She engaged Tessa with that line of thought; she was curious how her American background influenced her decision-making. Tessa was quick to agree, "It is difficult to succeed in male-dominated areas unless you screw them out of it, figuratively and literally. Just like your mother did."

Lee was caught off guard by the statement. It had never crossed her mind that Tessa would be privy to the information pertaining to her relationship with Blanch. Tessa saw the shocked look on Lee's face. "I am sorry if I spoke out of turn. I am guessing you weren't aware of my knowledge of your mother and her past." Tessa took Lee's silence as affirmation she didn't know.

Requesting another bottle of wine from the server, Tessa proceeded to share all the sordid details of Tessa's life and Blanch's involvement. She spoke of what a saint Lydia was for taking an interest in her and how she helped her survive the loss of her mother. "If it hadn't been for Lydia and Joanne, I don't think I would have survived through the legal battles that followed." Lee knew of the murder trials and her mothers assisting Tessa through the hard times but had no clue Blanch had been the root cause of the chaos. One more example of how vile the woman she came from was.

Tessa was straightforward with how she ostracized Blanch publicly any time the opportunity presented itself. Of all the things she shared over the next few hours, one tidbit caught Lee's attention the most. Hearing of Bobby's involvement with the scheme to take over the Fergus' company, this detail intrigued her. "I guess everyone has their Tino," Lee said out loud without thinking. Tessa begged pardon as she didn't understand what Lee meant by that.

As the bill arrived at the table, Tessa reached for her purse to pick up the check. Laying her credit card in the small silver tray, Tessa leaned back in the woven cane chair and smiled devilishly at Lee. "I think you should buy Murrel International and manufacture the products yourself. Rumor has it she is in serious financial trouble. If you don't have the means to purchase the company, I have connections that would be glad to invest."

Lee smiled back at her; without saying a word, she reached for Tessa's card and handed it back to her while placing euros in the tray. "They don't take credit cards here, and it is my pleasure spending time with you. I am not sure you know how much I adored Garret." Tessa took the piece of plastic from Lee before reaching to take her hand. Tears filled the soft laugh lines around her eyes; Tessa didn't say a word in response to Lee's adoration for her dead husband. Sitting there, holding hands, the unlikely duo became fast friends.

"Blanch is a mystery to me. Even though I carry her DNA, I don't understand her way of being. If I am honest with you, I am afraid of being like her." Tessa said she understood but believed

Gabriel's kindness and good looks were the more robust set of personality traits within Lee. "I didn't personally know him, but I do remember how charming he was. My mother gushed about how kind he was to her and hoped he would ask her to marry him after her divorce. My testimony at her murder trial is what put my father in prison. He turned into an awful man after discovering her infidelity. I have complete empathy for your not wanting to be like your parent." Lee did not challenge Tessa's fantasy of Gabriel's love for her mother; she kept his inability to love because of his past to herself.

With the last sip of wine consumed, the women parted ways with an agreement to stay in touch. Business cards with their personal phone numbers were exchanged, along with a promise to grow their newly forged friendship.

The sunset was just above the horizon as Lee crossed through the park to her apartment. Slightly drunk from the wine consumed with Tessa, she slowed her pace midway through the garden. Lee felt a need to slow down; she also wanted to process the suggestion Tessa made about her buying the factory. She was unsure if her new pal might be playing the revenge game as well. Lee did not want to be a pawn in someone else's desire to level the playing field and felt she had reason enough to get even with Blanch by herself. She didn't need outside influences pushing her to go back to her angry place.

The next morning, Tino waited for Lee with her usual latte at the front door of the office building. Sitting on the bench across the street, waiting for her for an unusual length of time. She was abnormally late, even by his standards. He had begun to worry about her just as her car pulled up in front of the bench he was residing on. Exiting the backseat, she stood tall and composed herself. Tino immediately knew she had not slept the night before; he had seen this look many times.

Handing her the drink without speaking, they moved across the street and up the stairs to the offices. Settling into her chair, the sunglasses came off, revealing swollen eyes from a night of crying. Tino closed the office doors before asking what was going on. "I had a message on my machine to call the Laverde's when I got home last night. Tia Maria passed away yesterday. I need to go to Madrid; I know it's not your job anymore, but I could really use your help."

Tino laid out a quick plan of tasks to be completed by each of them before he exited her office. He would make the transportation arrangements, and speak with her maid about what to pack. She was to reschedule any upcoming meetings. Lee moved into business mode very quickly, and few around the office could tell she was upset. She learned how to control her emotions in front of others over the years but was struggling with this event. She didn't know why but everything felt like it did when Jacque died. Maybe she really wasn't done mourning him.

Services followed the standard catholic rituals of which Lee knew little. She attended masses with the Laverdes previously, but it hadn't become a part of her. Growing up a Baptist in Texas formed her early views of organized religion, and she didn't consider any of it to be valid. Lydia would be disappointed in Lee's lack of faith, but for Lee, life had consistently reminded her no gods were providing her happiness. If they existed, she thought them to be cruel.

With the funeral over, Lee became eager to return to Paris and to work. Ernesto insisted she stayed through the end of the week with the family; she knew he was right. Lee had not visited with any of them since the last funeral they attended together. The family had been so good to her that she could not refuse the request; besides, Tino would phone her if anything critical occurred at the office.

The days passed quickly during her visit, and she was glad she had opted to stay with the family. She filled them in on her company and the impact she believed the brand would have on the world of dark-skinned people. The family was proud to see how she had matured and was becoming a person to be reckoned with.

On her last night in Madrid, she began to gather her things for packing. Piling the clothes on a chair for the maid to fold and pack, she found an envelope beneath the jewelry box on her dressing table. The return address was in Cali, Columbia. The envelope's contents were unknown as the envelope was still sealed, the address written in Gabriel's hand. Blanch's address in Dallas, TX, had been covered with bold letters; RETURN TO SENDER.

Lee left her room, holding the letter tightly between her fingers. She needed answers, and she knew who had them. Without even knocking, she entered her cousin's room. His being on his knees performing fellatio on the pool boy did not deter her from speaking. The sexy young pool boy, at least half Ernesto's age, scrambled to find something to cover himself with while Lee waved the envelope around, shouting questions at her cousin.

Rising to his feet, Ernesto dismissed the young man from the room while moving towards his bathroom to rinse out his mouth. Returning to where he had left Lee expressing herself, he was now in his dressing gown and moving towards a sofa. Motioning for her to sit, she finally stopped talking while crossing the room to be next to him. "I don't know what the contents are. As you can see, it was never opened. I found it on Tia's desk while preparing for her service. I can only assume it was with his belongings returned to the family after his passing. That is all I know."

Lee believed him and sat quietly, holding the letter. "Why was it just laid on my dressing table?" She wanted an answer and patiently waited for Ernesto to respond. Several minutes passed before he spoke. He didn't know how to address this with her; he had hopes she would not find the letter until she was back in Paris.

"You are aware of the drama between your father and the family. It was most unusual for my grandmother to take you in and treat you like you had always been around. None of us understood it. The fight within the family exploded in public when your father told everyone the truth about what Doña Laverde did. We assumed she was trying to save face." He went on to share other details of the family and how each of them had a high level of respect for their matriarch even though she had failed to protect her own. They believed she was grateful Lee had been sent to meet them; it kept the good part of Gabriel alive.

Ernesto had no explanation for why the letter had been put away and never read; he only surmised that his great-grandmother feared what information Gabriel was sharing with the woman who bore his child.

Lee softly stated, "It's marked return to sender, and the postmark is only a week before he died."

Both she and her cousin wondered what could have been so crucial that Gabriel would reach out to Blanch after so many years had passed. Lee shared her knowledge of her dad keeping in touch with Lydia, which was probably how he knew where Blanch was. "Is there anything good going to come from me reading this?" She waited for her cousin to respond before opening the letter. Ernesto's simple reply was to open it and find out.

Sitting quietly, thinking to herself while Ernesto crossed the room to fill two glasses with

Aguardiente. As he poured the liquid from the crystal decanter, she tore open the envelope and prepared to read the contents of the letter. Before Ernesto could return with the glasses of liquid sedative, Lee finished consuming the last words her father wrote. She took the glass from her cousin and, after drinking it in one gulp, requested another. Filling the glass as requested, Ernesto handed the warm liquid to Lee while taking the letter from her; he began his turn at finding out information he would have never imagined. Ernesto looked up from the letter, "He must have confided his illness to Abuela before he died. I wonder what prompted him to ask your mother to reconcile with you." Lee surmised her father was attempting to heal past wounds for his daughter.

Standing up, she looked her cousin in the eyes before speaking. "I had Tino go to Cali and research what really happened. He was unable to find anything other than Gabriel had visited his physician the morning of the boating accident."

Rereading the contents of the letter, the pair determined Gabriel had committed suicide.

His last act of selflessness was an attempt to ensure his daughter had a parent in her life.

"Perhaps if she had read his letter, she might have made an effort to find me. I would have been able to save him." Asking for a refill of the Aguardiente, Lee looked Ernesto in the eyes. "That bitch!"

CHAPTER 17

Blanch was caught by surprise to hear Lee on the other end of the phone. With the challenges she faced keeping the business afloat, she hadn't recently had time to pursue the Paris-based company. Seeing the writing on the wall, her staff had begun their exodus. Down to two salesmen, she spent her days attempting to keep the clients they had from leaving. Hearing the woman's French accent on the phone created hope in her that she had not felt for some time.

She readily agreed to have Lee's team visit the offices and factory to begin their due diligence. Blanch thought it odd Lee wanted to spend money auditing her company before they even came to terms on price. Based on the minimal information she had been able to gather thus far, the launch was intended for an international market. The initial orders necessary to fill the pipelines, by her estimation, should quickly generate over a million dollars in sales for Murrel; this would get her out of the immediate danger of closing the business. Her personal predictions for fulfilling a global market would generate ten times that amount annually. Blanch desperately needed to close this sale; she was in a bind and would bend in any way necessary to get this account. Her eagerness, evident to Lee, set the wheels in motion. Quickly proposing dates for the audit, Blanch felt a small sigh of relief.

The financial review was pristine; not one single late payment to her suppliers was noted. Lee knew this was false; obviously, the books were Blanch's personal set conjured up in anticipation of an audit. The ledgers prepared were for either a customer or an American IRS audit. Beyond the financial analysis, the French team reviewed all processes and procedures as protocol dictated. The serious issues with the quality assurance department brought huge concerns the manufacturer would never meet global compliance. European countries were far more advanced in their requirements than the US; this generated a great deal of concern for Lee's team. In addition to the systemic failures discovered, they couldn't understand why she wanted to produce products in

the US and ship them overseas. The transportation cost would grossly impact the bottom line.
This choice was a mystery even to Tino.

When the final reports were provided to
Blanch's team in a formal review meeting, the
outcome was grim. Blanch did not attend the
meeting, which was a clear sign to Lee she was on
the right trajectory for what she wanted. She asserted her birth mother needed time to create
whatever excuse was necessary for the shortcomings. Near the conclusion of the meeting, Lee requested Blanch join the meeting; she wanted to
observe the reaction of the woman who had
birthed her.

Entering the room, Blanch was already
flush with anger at being summoned. The red
blotchy skin, sans makeup to hide her emotions,
tipped Lee off that Blanch's team had already told
their boss the reports were not good. Blanch covered up so many things over the years that it was
inevitable something she didn't want to admit
would be uncovered. Walking past the empty
chair at the head of the table, Blanch took the seat

to the left of it. She believed this to be a power play, it softened her approach, or so she perceived. This was a ploy she learned from Joanne Fergus.

Lee smiled at the woman at the other end of the table, which put Blanch at ease. Lee wasn't smiling to comfort Blanch; she was smiling to hide her internal laughter at the games played in the boardroom. She had arrived at the conclusion it didn't really matter the gender of the person who was running the business; the actual qualifier for success was what one was willing to do to win.

Lee sat quietly while Blanch's employees outlined the issues that had been set out before them. In every case, Blanch had a reason for why any failure had occurred. Never once did she allow her team to speak beyond conveying the shortcomings of their group. Blanch was incredibly adept at explaining issues away. She most often used tactics of diversion in an attempt to sway the focus to something else, hoping the initial issue being discussed would be forgotten. She called it the Squirrel Game. When all was said and done,

Lee requested the group exit and leave her and Blanch to discuss the events from the past four days.

Blanch excused herself with her team, stating she wanted to retrieve pen and paper. Lee suspected she was up to something but intended to further her plan. Tino inquired if everyone on the EU team should wait or move on without Lee. Looking at her watch, she determined they had four hours to kill before the team needed to be at the airport for their flight back to Paris. She had plans to stay in Dallas for a few more days and thought it best to send them on without her. "Take everyone to a nice bit of an early dinner before you go to the airport. They deserve it. I will be back in the office on Monday and will update everyone on my decisions at that time. Au revoir." Tino nodded yes and excused himself from the room. Lee noted that his path led towards Bobby's desk and not to the front lobby. She assumed he wanted to say goodbye to his playmate.

Blanch returned to the meeting room, suggesting to Lee they make their way to her office in order to be more comfortable. Gathering up her notepad and bag, she dutifully followed Blanch through the rows of cubicles and into the office. Sitting on the soft leather chair in front of the desk, she motioned for Lee to sit in the chair opposite her, subtly implying the conversation should be a friendly one. Lee kicked off her shoes and placed one leg on the seat of the chair before sitting. Once she was situated in the seat, the other leg was raised and crossed over, creating a very zen pose. A casual response to Blanch's request. Blanch was impressed by the women's flexibility and subtly released a deeply held breath. It appeared the two of them were on the same page.

"I think the best place for us to start is to ask you how much equity are you willing to part with?" Blanch's eyes opened wide; she was shocked by what Lee asked. How dare this woman assume her company was up for sale. Once again, the redness of her skin gave her away, and Lee saw no reason to not proceed with her idea. "As much as you have tried to hide it, I know you have financial issues. Rumor has it your equity partners are looking for an exit strategy. I think we can help each other out."

Blanch rose from her seat, no longer sensing this was a chat amongst girlfriends. As she paced around her office, she denied the assertion made by Lee. Her ten-minute rant did not generate a response from her audience; this was unusual as Blanch had always been able to rile the emotions of others. It was not working on this girl; she couldn't understand the lack of response from Madame de Leon.

Eventually giving in to the lack of engagement, Blanch sat in her desk chair while looking across it at the woman in her office. Sensing the diatribe was over, Lee unfurled her legs and leaned back in the chair.

"Based on your tirade, I see you are not open to a partnership. You have significant deficiencies in every department except for finance, which is probably explained by your background and development of the finance group. The only way I would be able to do business with you is if I had some control over the decision-making process. It appears that is not an option for you. I will bid you adieu." Finishing her statement, Lee reached for her belongings and slipped her feet into her shoes lying on the floor. Without any further comment, Lee exited the room. Passing Bobby's desk, she wished him a good day.

Sitting in the handcrafted leather chair, she had personally designed, Blanch could not make heads nor tails out of what had just happened. She had not felt like this since she was a young girl being scolded by her mother. When Bobby entered the room, she didn't even notice him placing her perfectly filled cup of ice and diet soda on her desk. Blanch was in shock; she had always been able to talk her way around a roadblock until now. She had to develop a new plan of attack.

Waking up refreshed, Lee was ready to take the next step in her plan. Even though it was Saturday morning, she had a lunch meeting scheduled. A meeting she was slightly anxious about. A discussion that would have major implications for her new business venture.

She arrived shortly before her lunch companion at the restaurant, allowing her time to peruse the wine list. In the ways of her European forefathers, Lee did not think it unseemly to have wine at a business lunch. She found the puritanical rituals making their way into the American corporate scene odd. At the pace the culture was changing, the liquor cabinets would all be removed from the CEO's offices by the end of the millennium.

Sipping on her Pinot Grigio, she patiently waited for her guest to arrive. Finally, she saw Tessa being escorted to their table. Greeting each other with kisses on the cheeks, they quickly settled into an afternoon of fine food and conversation. Lee confirmed the suspicions about Murrel International's financial challenges. Tessa was unable to stop smiling while hearing of the ongoing issues found during the audit. More importantly, she was ecstatic to hear the books had been altered, concealing the actual status of the business. Tessa continued to grin at the prospect of Blanch Murrel getting what she deserved.

"I will set everything in motion, and I promise you by the end of next week, Blanch Murrel will phone you with an equity offer," Tessa assured Lee that Blanch would never allow the Fergus Family to get their hands back on the business, regardless of what she had to give up. She was positive the suggestion of a buyout from Joanne would send the current owner heading in the exact direction they wanted. Finishing their wine and small bits of lunch, Tessa suggested the women spend the afternoon shopping at the Galleria.

Other than the tiring eleven-hour flight from Dallas, Lee's trip home was uneventful. She did not like flying overnight as she could never sleep on a plane, but even more so, she had tired of the connections required between Dallas and New York to Paris. The two hours of flight time saved by flying the Concorde was not worth the hassle any longer. She preferred to spend her time in the air in one seat, reading books and reviewing business plans.

After dinner, she attempted to contact Tino via the air phone at her seat. After three times being disconnected and not managing to get beyond saying hello to him, she resigned herself to relax. She put her paperwork away and ordered a Grey Goose Martini while beginning to read a new book, "Deathbed Confession." She was surprised when she woke to the crew serving breakfast on the plane. Lee couldn't recall ever falling asleep on a plane before; she surmised it must have been the cocktail.

Tino greeted her at the gate and escorted her home just as he had done for many years. Mostly, he was anxious to hear what the plan was with the US-based manufacturer. If they were to meet their launch dates less than six months out, they needed a clear direction for where the products would be manufactured. Lee told him she wasn't able to commit to a decision just yet. "I am confident we will resolve the issues with the facility in Texas. If we are not able to, I have a backup plan."

She thanked Tino for his work in discovering the critical information she needed. Tino smiled and told her it was his pleasure, literally. "Bobby really is a nice man; I wouldn't have thought it, but I enjoyed the time spent with him." Lee was amused at how gay men appeared to view sex as a pastime; she considered the notion it was probably just men, gay or straight. She was also very thankful that Bobby still enjoyed his pillow talk about his boss.

Tessa called Lee late Wednesday afternoon to update her on what had transpired between the current and former owners of the manufacturing company. Tessa shared how Joanne told Blanch of her conversations with a few friends and her discovery of the dire straits Murrel International was truly in. "Blanch exploded at Joanne for suggesting her company was in trouble. Blanch claimed it was all lies and everything with the company was in perfect order."

The following day, as Tessa predicted, Blanch called Lee to suggest they create a partnership. Lee requested Blanch send over a proposal from Murrel International outlining the percentage of equity and positions to be held. Agreeing to submit the proposal by the end of the week, the two disconnected their call, both very pleased with themselves.

Being crafty as she was, Blanch included a few provisions within the proposal tying Le Peau Sombre to the factory for an extended period of time. This was unexpected by Lee but fit with her long-term vision. Blanch had not expected Lee to insist on a board of directors consisting of members from both companies; she quickly let her concern go as soon as Lee clarified Señor Alvarez would be included on the board.

Each company's legal team reviewed and word-smithed the final details within a few weeks. Soon, Lee would be president of Murrel International and own forty-two percent of the organization. In turn, Le Peau Sombre would be the primary account for Murrel International and, specifically, its DBA, Fergus Manufacturing, guaranteed production for the next ten years.

Le Peau Sombre was also insured their products would be produced at cost plus ten percent during that time. This was great for their cost model and bottom line; Lee's team had a new respect for her ability to manage such a fantastic cost structure.

When hired by Lee, a team member was promised a bonus based on bottom-line savings each year; their boss just guaranteed them bonuses for the rest of their employment by implementing this agreement.

Blanch was on a high as she had made the deal that would save the company and ultimately keep it out of the hands of the Fergus family forever. With the hidden cost she had built into the product quotes, she expected to build up funds unknown to her new partner. The intent was to generate cash fast enough to buy back the equity she sold to Lee and take over the French skincare company within five years.

In Blanch's mind, the hotshot French businesswoman would never know what hit her. She had also worked out a side benefit of Tino serving on the board of directors.

CHAPTER 18

The following eight months sped by for both companies. Lee split her time between Dallas and Paris; as president of Murrel International, she had to ensure her presence was felt. She found herself sliding back into her native East Texas mannerisms and had to constantly remind herself to stay "French" in her speech and her actions.

As CEO, Blanch managed Lee behind the scenes reviewing each of her decisions; no alterations at the company were implemented without her consent. The staff learned early on to confirm directives from Lee with their big boss before proceeding, all except for Finance which was kept out of reach from Lee.

Blanch placed a new CPA in the role of Chief Financial Officer just before Lee took her position with the group; Blanch expected complete loyalty from the new hire. The gentleman had no idea what he was getting into. With Blanch's promise of sexual favors, anytime he asked, he was under her complete control.

Lee was quite savvy, but her lack of finance knowledge left her in the position of not always knowing what questions to ask. This was precisely what Blanch had hoped for.

The scale-up processes of the new cosmetics line continued forward with challenges. The French R&D team had been incredibly proficient in preparing the transfer files from their lab to the factory in Dallas. The issues arising were consistently due to the failures of Blanch's team members.

Blanch ostracized her leadership each time a failure occurred, often saying their bonuses had just been flushed down the drain. Attempting to conceal as much as possible from Lee, Bobby had been given specific instructions that meetings would only occur when the President of Murrel was off-site. Hearing how her birth mother shamed her staff in front of their team members, Lee smiled, knowing this behavior would lead the staff to become endeared to her over the long haul.

The staff at Le Peau Sombre referred to the team at the factory as Peu À Propos, a French idiom suggesting their American counterparts were inept. Sharing their concerns with their leader, Lee would defend the American workers saying the steep learning curve would soon be overcome. Lee would address the issues with Blanch, always accepting the reasons why something failed. Filing the information away in her personal book of records that even Tino didn't have access to.

Lee's lawyers had been wise to insert verbiage in the contract between the two companies stating Murrel would cover all costs related to production failures. Even though this impacted the company Lee served as President, it protected Le Peau Sombre from unexpected chargebacks.

Storefronts in Europe were on schedule and would be ready for the launch of the line as planned. Lee personally selected the store locations in Barcelona, Madrid, Paris, Monte Carlo, and New York. They would launch the stores simultaneously using the latest technology. The primary launch site would be the Monte Carlo store. Live feeds to each of the remaining locations would broadcast the festivities to the other stores via closed-circuit television. Madame de Leon was highly pleased with how her marketing company created excitement around the new skincare line; "Created for women around the world!" was the tagline.

Returning to Dallas for a company board meeting, Lee was caught off guard at Blanch's off-putting disposition. Blanch did her best to keep her brave face on in front of the new business partner and President of her company, but she had bad news to deliver to Le Peau Sombre before the leadership team gathered the following day. Blanch avoided eye contact with Lee, desperately looking for a way to alter the message to lessen its impact, but she could not find one. Not only was the information she had to share with her leadership team hurtful to her most significant customer, but it would also impact her financial plans as well.

After an invitation to dinner and cocktails had been suggested by Blanch, Lee closed the door to the owner's office and sat down in the leather chair across from her birth mother. Declining the invitation to dine, Lee proceeded to point blank ask what was going on. The familiar red skin of irritation quickly covered Blanch's face. She looked at the carpet in front of Lee for at least five minutes before responding. Lee never changed her position in the chair once; she just sat patiently, waiting for Blanch to speak. "We're a family now; I think that is why this is so hard to say. I think of you as a daughter if I had ever had one, so please try to not be irritated when you hear what I have to say."

Lee sat quietly, listening to the words, internally cringing at the realization her birth mother did not have a single notion the girl sitting across from her was, indeed, her offspring.

The news of the purchasing department's error was delivered; incorrect packaging for the product line had been ordered and received. In addition, the wrong artwork had been printed on each bottle. To add insult to injury, no one noticed until the materials were delivered to the production area for processing. There would be no prod-uct available for the opening.

Lee did not react; she was still focused on Blanch's attempt to smooth things over by play-ing the family card. Fully aware of the statement's irony, she couldn't help but think of the family in Madrid and Lydia. These people understood the value of relationships; the juxtaposition between her birth mother's narcissistic behavior and the people who had given her so much was never more apparent.

Waiting for Lee to respond, a nervous ener-gy began to build in Blanch. The combination of her investment in the company and the money it would lose if Lee chose to enforce provisions with-in their contract, she would lose bigger than she ever hoped to win.

"What are our options to resolve this chal-lenge?" was all that came out of Lee's mouth. Blanch wasn't prepared for this; she expected a tirade from the French diva. "You said we were family; family helps each other find a path for-ward. What solutions has the team identified for resolution?" Her voice never quivered or increased in volume; she played the part of the leader and family member to perfection.

Their afternoon was quickly filled with meetings and phone calls to vendors for solutions. In each and every case, the Murrel team attempted to place blame on the vendor for the problems facing them. Lee always shut down the blame game, stating that who was at fault was not here nor there. The charming French woman won the vendors' hearts by focusing on resolution instead of beating them up for something they had no control over. The Murrel team despised this approach; they were used to the Blanch method of beating people down, reminding them who the customer was and, therefore, always right.

By the time the leadership team met the following day, a solution was in place. Lee quietly waited for Tino's response after it was announced the skincare launch would be delayed by one month. She kept her eyes firmly on Blanch when he began to speak. "This will impact Sombre significantly. We are now paying rent on space in major buildings in key cities in both Europe and the US. The cost to reset the broadcast, reprint the media, etc., could easily reach a hundred thousand US dollars. We will have no choice but to charge that back to Murrel."

It was in the contract; Murrel would have no choice but to pay it back. All the money she expected to make would be wiped out in one swoop. She appeared to have temporarily left her body; she just stared at Tino, utterly unaware of her child observing her. The other board members and the executive team sat motionless; they knew the impact of what had happened and the realization that each of them may soon be without a position or income.

Lee interrupted the silence, "As I sit in a responsible position for both companies, I believe we can find a solution that will not bankrupt Murrel and soften the financial impact on Sombre."

Blanch mentally returned to the room when hearing Lee's suggestion. Just as Lee had suspected, Blanch was acting out the scene from Comatose 1, the movie. Lee smiled at everyone and suggested they continue on with the status of the company as planned for the meeting. "We are all in this together; let's not lose focus on the end game." Blanch leaned back in her chair; her planned speech about family and sticking together had worked. She had played this one right!

Lee and Tino giggled to themselves; no other person in the room caught on to their ruse. Their performance was flawless; everything had been preplanned. Lee was fully aware of the issue before arriving in Dallas; Tino's part-time lover had previously faxed the details to the Paris office.

As was traditional, the group gathered for a meal at an upscale restaurant after the meeting. It was intended to be a time to build relationships and reward everyone in leadership for their hard work. Tino found it odd how Americans separated the working classes; he felt it lacked respect for the common man. This was just one of the many differences in work philosophies between the countries. Of course, he didn't really mind as long as he benefited in the end.

Blanch did not thank Lee for her suggestion to find a plan that evening. It wasn't until someone else at dinner saluted her bravery and brilliance for saving both companies Blanch felt compelled to repeat her diatribe of what being a family means. She went on to add the collaboration was simply a part of the Murrel culture. After Blanch finished her speech, Lee rose from her chair, graciously accepting the applause of appreciation. "I am not acting a hero; I never said Murrel won't repay Sombre for the failure, only that we focus on the end game for now. Payback will be long-term so both companies can continue to operate; we will need to determine a plan once we understand all the costs." Lee smiled over her martini at Blanch. She knew Blanch would not react in front of the group; she could not afford to.

"Tino and the Sombre team will gather the information regarding the costs of the setback by the next quarterly meeting. At that time, we can discuss how to proceed in each company's best interest." Once again, Lee was ahead of Blanch; she was completely aware of the hidden profit taken on the cost of goods. She knew the inflated cost would only further impact the loss to Murrel. Blanch would have to come clean about the deception one way or another.

Tino and Bobby were brilliant at keeping their personal relationship quiet, and Bobby was unaware his loose lips served more than one master. Even if he had known Tino was passing the information on to his boss, it wouldn't have mattered. Not knowing Tino was sharing the information with her left him looking foolish to Lee. She couldn't help but feel sorry for him being taken advantage of, and she didn't know why.

As time passed, Bobby's resentment of the manner in which Blanch treated him grew stronger every day. From the occasional gay slur to the refusal to provide him a fair salary, Bobby had grown tired of being used. Never adequately rewarded for the job he did, he grew to understand what kind of person Blanch was and often thought about leaving. But somehow, a promise of a future reward for all his hard work helped prolong his making an exit. He hoped that one day,

Lee would see his value and make up for what he had missed out on.

Lee pushed the Murrel staff daily to meet their commitments; it appeared the launch for Sombre would meet the delayed date. The time-line was dangerously tight, leaving no margin of error for either company. Blanch disliked Lee's pushing but remained silent as it was in her best interest, for the moment being. She thought Señor Alvarez was the better option to resolve the challenges at hand.

Tino thought Blanch to be manipulative and vile; he often called her Cruela behind her back. Taking great pleasure in the thought she would fail, he hoped it would end with a big splat! He had his plans for the future and was quietly working in the background to ensure his financial success. He had his personal reason for capturing every chargeback found; he intended to capture every cent. Tino assumed when Murrel became a subsidiary of Sombre; he would take on the role of President at the factory. He never discussed this assumption with Lee; he asserted it was a given based on his long-term commitment to her. He also maintained a log of all the insider information her had gathered just in case he had to force her hand to get what he wanted.

He didn't know what Lee's issue was with Blanch, and he didn't really care. He was busy laying out his financial plans for the future, plans that would alter significantly after an evening of cocktails with the CEO of Murrel International.

All the opposing forces and manipulations were beginning to wear on Lee. She found herself in a position of not trusting the people around her. As long as she had known Tino, she was aware of his behavioral patterns and learned to keep an eye on him. The similarities between him and Blanch were lost on her. She could sense they didn't care for each other, and she accepted this as a part of life. She also sensed not everything was as it appeared on the surface.

Taking time from her busy schedule to visit the storefronts and ensure everything met her expectations, she met with Ernesto for dinner while in Madrid. They began the evening touring the new store before making their way to dinner, just the two of them. She had promised to stay the weekend with the family at Pozuelo de Laverde but wanted this time alone with her cousin.

Ernesto was quick to see the shift in Lee; she was no longer the fun-loving, sweet girl who had arrived at his family's home years before. Their relationship had been built on honesty and the ability to discuss anything; he didn't waste any time telling her he was worried about who she was becoming. At first, Lee resented him saying it out loud. Then she realized he was correct in his assessment; she was shifting and felt as if she was losing her way.

Their evening ran long into the night; for the first time in months, Lee did not talk about business. Although Lee loved being the successful business women she was becoming, Ernesto's comments regarding her personality shift reminded her she must be cautious to not lose her soul. It was with the third glass of Cabernet she told her cousin the truth about what she was doing and the involvement with her birth mother.

Ernesto listened carefully while Lee revealed her anger and the need to get even with Blanch. She went on to confess it was after she received the letter he found in Tia Maria's belongings that triggered her into action.

As she shared information with him, the pieces of the puzzle were coming together. Taking all the details in, he was becoming very concerned for her well-being as well as her financial future. He knew all too well what kinds of tricks Tino pulled on people. The jewelry stolen from Doña Laverde was not the first issue he had with Tino. He was grateful when Lee forced Tino's hand with the stolen pendant; it gave him the courage to stop financially supporting Tino without any significant consequences. He assumed Lee had figured Tino out; apparently, his assessment was incorrect.

Lee continued bringing him up to speed with everything going on in her life, and the more he heard, he realized he had to intervene. "What if the businesses fail, either of them? What will you do?" Lee noticed the concern in his voice when he asked the question. Patting him on the hand, "The Laverde and de Leon money are safely put away if that is what you are referencing." Her tone left Ernesto feeling as if she thought he was questioning her judgment; he was, in a way. It was then he said the words needed to lift the veil covering her eyes, "Tino and Blanch are two of a kind. They are both narcissistic manipulators, and you are playing on the same playground with both of them. Beware."

Lee was dumbfounded by his statement; she could not disagree with his observation. He was absolutely right. "What is wrong with me? I have put myself in the position of getting hurt again. Merde!"

The epiphany was instant; she realized she had kept Tino by her side all these years because he was just like her birth mother. How had she not recognized the familiarity of being a convenience, cast aside when it suited him? She could not allow herself to be hurt like that again. Exiting the restaurant on her cousin's arm, her cell phone rang. She refused the call and turned the device off. She declined all communications from Blanch or Tino for the rest of the weekend. She would make the most of her time with her father's family in Madrid.

CHAPTER 19

Lee completed her tour of the stores in Europe; New York was the last on her list as it was on her way back to Dallas. Arriving at the 5th Avenue location, she was surprised to find Tino there. Lee wasn't ready to see him just yet; she needed to sort out the craziness in her mind and find a path to remove herself from both him and her birth mother.

Tino's responses towards her were very curt from the first moment they spoke; perhaps it was her recent revelation that made his behavior appear rude. Maybe he had always been that way, and she had never noticed. It was most likely the fact, in her mind, he now resembled Blanch in every way.

The unscheduled meeting between the two of them managed to remain somewhat polite during their time together in SoHo, but when asked to go uptown for drinks, Lee begged off, claiming she had to get back to the office in Dallas. She was surprised he relinquished the invitation so quickly as he always knew every detail in regard to her travel plans. Tino knew something was up.

Awaking to her cellular phone ringing the next morning, Lee was abrupt when answering it. She had forgotten to turn it off the night before when she went to bed. She hated having a phone with her twenty-four-seven, and now it had disturbed the very small amount of sleep she had managed to get.

"I hope I didn't wake you. I didn't think about you being jet lagged." It was Blanch on the other end of the connection. Before waiting for a response, Blanch continued speaking, "I received the preliminary numbers from Tino, and I don't know how we will manage a payback scenario. I am just not sure how." Lee was again feeling the pressures of her newfound knowledge. Instead of saying the words forming in her mind, she flipped the phone closed and pushed the 'Off' button. She was unprepared for the conversation with Blanch regarding the financial matter or anything else.

The surprise call leaving her fully awake forced her to make her way to the bathroom to prepare for the day. Lee knew she couldn't leave Blanch hanging like she had; there were too many issues that could arise if she wasn't careful. Finishing her continental breakfast, she retrieved the portable phone. Flipping the lid up, Lee turned the phone back on and pushed the speed dial button for Blanch. Answering on the first ring, she was quite short with Lee. Lee apologized, explaining her phone battery had died and that, in her jet-lagged state, she had not thought to use the landline before falling back to sleep. Adding credibility to the lie, she told Blanch she had forgotten to charge the phone when she went to bed.

Lee quickly noticed how fast Blanch's mood shifted with the excuse of a dead battery. Each new interaction with her mother brought insight into what she had been missing through the years. She felt foolish that she had never noticed any of this before. Jacque had told her numerous times he didn't care for Tino, but nothing more. He never offered any insight as to why and never made her feel bad or ashamed of who her friend was. In hindsight, she now understood the reasons behind why her sweet husband didn't trust

Tino. She was now even more grateful she followed his guidance regarding Tino having access to her funds. She then began to wonder if he would be brazen enough to forge her signature; he had access to Sombre's bank accounts, after all.

Focusing back on her mother, she asked Blanch to calm down as they would find a solution to the issue when she arrived in the office that afternoon. "I don't understand why you are coming back to Dallas when we have to be in Monte Carlo in three days." Lee knew what Blanch was hinting at; she didn't want Lee back at the plant to dig into the additional production losses. One more revelation for Lee to file away, another debate to be had with her inner voice on what she should do.

Originally this plan had begun with the intent to punish Blanch for what happened with Gabriel. The more she thought about the unread letter, she pondered if things might have played out differently if Blanch had not returned it unopened.

Now, aware of the subconscious choices driving her life, she wasn't sure she could follow through with the plan. She was being pulled in multiple directions; Tessa and Joanne gunning for Blanch, Tino, and Bobby up to something in the background; they were all using her to get even with the woman who never wanted her as a child.

Processing all this information on the way to the Dallas office, it occurred to Lee that Blanch appeared to be the common denominator in this chaos she was caught up in. Thinking back to what her therapist had said about cognitive observances, she admitted her anger against her mother led her to this moment in time. How she chose to move forward would define who she really was as a person.

Placing her purse on the chair in her office, she proceeded back into the corridor and made her way around the corner to Bobby's desk. She usually didn't engage with him very much; she didn't want to accidentally say something he assumed only Tino would know. The time had come for her to discover Bobby's level of involvement with Tino.

The thought had crossed her mind that both he and Tino had access to her signature and could very easily forge her name on Sombre checks alongside Tino's. She trusted her business accountant in France, and nothing had ever surfaced about unusual expenditures within her holdings. But now, she found herself not believing in anyone, including herself.

Bobby smiled at her while making small talk before she opened the can of worms necessary to see what he knew. "I wanted to say thank you for the paperwork showing the hidden fees within the purchasing group. It is going to be very useful in the near future." She watched the smile slide from his face; that told her all she needed to know. Bobby was not aware the information being shared with Tino was passed on to her. "Merci, Beaucoup!" bounced across her lips as she walked away.

Looking over her shoulder, back to where Bobby's desk was, she was not surprised to see him on the phone, white as a ghost. She could only assume he was speaking with Tino; the final round of games had begun. She made a mental note to call her lawyer and her accountant at Sombre just as soon as she was done with Blanch. All transactions going forward would require her approval.

Blanch's door was closed, but that did not stop Lee from entering the office after a single knock on her door. Her birth mother was not in her office chair as Lee was expecting. Moving past the desk, Lee sat in the overstuffed chair. Soaking it all in, she was interrupted when Blanch flushed the toilet in her private bathroom. Lee had ample time to move out of the comfortable chair but opted to wait and see the look on Blanch's face when she found her colleague in her seat.

"I didn't realize you had made it back already." The familiar irritation showing on her pale skin, she made her way to her chair while motioning with her hands for Lee to vacate it. As a good daughter should, Lee turned the chair towards Blanch and left it vacant for the company's

CEO. Taking a seat, Blanch reached for her phone and dialed Bobby's extension; it was busy. "You can wait for me here while I go to the kitchen and refill my beverage. I am a bit parched." Lee acknowledged the statement by nodding yes, continuing to stand beside the CEO's desk.

Blanch perceived Lee standing as a power play. Staying in the executive kitchen, she took an excessive amount of time to prepare her beverage. It was her chance to play a control card; Lee would just have to wait on her. Finally returning to her office, she noticed Bobby was still on the phone and appeared overly frustrated. She would deal with that issue later; for now, she needed to focus on what Lee wanted. Returning to her office, she discovered it was empty. Lee was not there.

Taking a sip of her diet soda, she pondered why Lee had not waited for her. Internally she didn't perceive Lee as a manipulator; perhaps she misread the signs. Leaving the refreshment on her desk, Blanch exited the office in search of Lee. Lee was not visible amongst the room full of cubicles, and her office was empty. Looking around the President's office for signs indicating where she might have gone, Blanch noticed the high heel shoes by the edge of Lee's desk revealing where she had gone.

Pushing open the door that linked the main offices to the manufacturing floor, her pace increased while searching for Lee. From Blanch's perspective, it was risky for Lee to engage with anyone on the production team; these people would have no clue what was inappropriate to share with her, and if the President of the company asks a question, logic says you should answer. Rounding a corner, she found Lee standing next to a pallet of Sombre products. Blanch released a huge sigh; Lee was only chatting with a warehouse employee. Seeing Blanch in the reflection of a safety mirror above the warehouse manager's desk, she turned to face Blanch before speaking. "The New York store was short on stock; glad to see it is leaving today." Turning back to the manager, "I need the manifest for the shipments that were air freighted to the EU locations before the end of the day. Thank you." Walking towards Blanch, she smiled while admitting she was being overly diligent as she didn't want to risk any store running out of stock. This allowed Blanch to relax even more; Lee was, as she had expected, a simple woman with money who took her work very seriously.

Back through the office doors, Blanch followed Lee into her office and questioned what she had come to see her for. "I wanted to follow up with you on your conversation with Tino regarding the payback scenario to Sombre. I want all business out of the way before we head to the launch party. The event should consist of nothing but fun and be full of surprises."

Blanch did not want to have this conversation but knew it was unavoidable. Lee pulled a chart from her LV briefcase and handed it to Blanch. The costs were neatly laid out, with the payback of losses applied. The cost Lee had listed in the chart was a perfect match for the amount Blanch had been pilfering with the fake vendor invoices.

For two years going forward, Murrel International would apply a discount to outbound shipments until the losses Sombre incurred were recovered. "With this approach, we can continue manufacturing without killing the cash flow of the business." Blanch immediately observed the line items showing the actual cost along with the internal markup. She wondered how Lee could have known the vendor was providing a kickback to Murrel. She couldn't ask the question as it would confirm guilt on her part. If word was to get out she had been cooking the books, the customers whose orders covered the operating cost of the business would evaporate.

Blanch was confused by Lee's approach; she had presented a path to protect the future of product production but killed an opportunity to recover the investment made in Murrel at the beginning of their partnership.

Blanch had been cautious to keep the outsider equity low enough the company couldn't be taken over. In her mind, if Lee were attempting to take over the company, she would have forced bankruptcy on Murrel; she would have forced the issue when she had the chance, exactly as Blanch had done with Joanne Fergus.

Blanch was unaware that if Le Peau Sombre was successful, the discount plan would recoup Lee's initial investment into her company by the end of the second year of sales. Apparently, Blanch wasn't the only one who knew how to be creative with numbers. It was Joanne Fergus' brilliance that created the payback plan for Lee.

As part of the payback plan, Lee insisted Murrel International restructure, creating a separate business entity in Fergus Manufacturing. Fergus must also align with another facility with similar capabilities should a disaster recovery be required. She would not let Sombre suffer from an unforeseeable stunt that Blanch might enact. Again, Blanch had no choice. If she didn't comply with Lee's requirements, she would lose the business and could quite possibly go to jail for fraud. Blanch finally agreed to Sombre's demands, telling Lee she would send the information via email to the CFO and legal. She would CC Lee on the correspondence. She then asked for a copy of the chart's data file. Lee agreed to send the file to her electronically before the end of the day.

With all the business behind them, Blanch, Lee, and Bobby were heading for the south of France. Bobby was in attendance to assist with anything Blanch might need. Lee had made it a point to personally "invite" Bobby for that reason. At the check-in counter, Lee overheard Bobby had been assigned a seat in coach. She graciously interrupted the gate agent, requesting an upgrade to business class for the long journey. Furthering his confusion about what was transpiring in the background, she patted Bobby on the arm. "A simple payback for all that you have done for me." Using her personal card for the additional fee, Blanch couldn't intervene as it was not her money. Lee knew this would drive Blanch mad, wondering what Bobby had been doing for Lee. What transaction had Bobby enacted that pushed Lee to treat him to business class?

This was indeed a perk for Bobby and just one of many Lee had planned for him. He entertained the thought he had endeared himself to

Lee, which might be good for his future based on recent events. What he didn't think about was Blanch's realization of where Lee obtained the numbers presented in the reimbursement plan.

On the plane bound for Europe, the two executives sat adjacent to each other in first class. Blanch ignored Lee as best she could. Her complete focus on reading books, scanning through them so fast it was improbable she would retain the details of their storylines. Lee enjoyed her food and beverage service conversing entirely in Spanish with the attendant. Blanch finally broke her silence by asking how many languages did Lee speak. Lee politely responded that she spoke four fluently and a few others at a beginner's level. Watching Lee interacting with the flight attendant in Spanish sparked a memory for her. She recognized something in Lee she had never seen before, but she could not make sense of what it was. Lee noticed Blanch's reading slowed as she appeared lost, deep in thought.

Finally arriving in Monte Carlo, the travelers dispersed to their accommodations to rest.

Lee apologized to Blanch and Bobby for putting them in a hotel instead of her apartment; she explained there would be many people coming and going at her home, which would not allow Blanch much peace and quiet. Blanch did not mind staying in the hotel at Lee's expense; she preferred to be sequestered away from everyone as much as possible anyway.

Arriving at Hôtel de Paris, Blanch was escorted to a room located next door to Bobby. She was not thrilled to be so close to her assistant in the hotel but decided being nearby allowed her to keep an eye on him. She wasn't sure if he was deliberately betraying her or not, but she was definitely going to find out.

Her room was adequate, but it was certainly not one of the premium suites; she was disappointed, to say the least. Bobby, on the other hand, was thrilled to be staying in any room at the establishment. On the elevator ride up to their floor, he shared his knowledge of the hotel and its use in a James Bond film. Blanch was not impressed with his familiarity with the hotel and was focused on his perceived betrayal. Before this trip was over, she would find out what information he had shared with Lee.

Exiting the lift, she commanded he be ready for dinner in four hours; they would be dining together that evening. Bobby had other plans but knew he couldn't ignore his boss's directive. He confirmed he would meet her in the lobby and reminded her the hotel demanded black-tie dress after six o'clock.

At first, she didn't recognize her assistant sitting at the bar. In his Armani tuxedo with velvet lapels and braids, Bobby's appearance had been elevated. His sense of style never bothered her; she just figured he wore what he could afford on the salary she paid him. Seeing him in a costume that easily cost more than a month's salary added to her suspicions. She, in her simple black cocktail dress, paled in comparison to him. Her hair was perfectly pulled up into a bun showcasing the stunning canary diamond studs weighing in at a karat on each ear. Bobby did not expect to see her with such lavish jewelry. He had never seen her wear anything beyond a ruby ring with tiny diamonds on her right hand and a stainless steel watch on her left wrist.

Reaching the barstool where Bobby was waiting, the bartender presented Blanch with a French 75. She recalled why she had held on to Bobby for so long; he remembered the little details that made her happy. "Your tuxedo is quite fetching." Blanch left the statement at that, expecting he would likely tell her its origin. "A gift from Madame de Leon," was all he said.

About to order another round of drinks, they were interrupted by a beautiful young woman who worked for the hotel; she informed them their car was waiting out front for them. "I will take care of your bill, madame, and monsieur, Bonsoir." They turned to each other and smiled before strolling through the iron doors under the metal awning. Moving down the steps to the Rolls Royce waiting for them, they felt as if they were royalty. Once inside the luxurious car, Blanch turned to Bobby and inquired where they were going to dine. He stared at her with a surprised look. "I assumed you arranged this; I didn't." A moment of panic set in as they realized they willingly entered into a car, not knowing where they were going or who was covering the cost. The chauffeur tilted his head slightly to the right before informing them Monsieur Alvarez had made the arrangements, and they would be dining with him that evening.

Tino had not intended to dine with either of them that night; he had plans with one of his many lovers. That engagement was postponed when Lee told him to entertain the two since her family was in town. He would have typically found a way out of her request, but this time he graciously agreed as he didn't know exactly what she had said to Bobby when she was in Texas. He only knew Bobby was frazzled after Lee arrived at the corporate offices. Tino also didn't know how much information Blanch had about the two of them. This was a chance to quiz the duo and have an expensive dinner on Lee's expense account. He was not yet aware his financial privileges were in the process of being revoked.

Enjoying their Michelin Star meal at Le Louis XV, Tino was interrupted by a man Blanch thought she knew. He excused himself for interrupting in English before utilizing his native tongue to converse with Tino. Blanch stared at the man, her jaw slightly ajar. When seeing him walk towards the table, she believed it was Gabriel coming to speak to her. Bobby noticed the odd gaze on her face and questioned if she was all right; at first glance, he thought she might be having a stroke. She responded that she was fine. After the conversation ended, the man told each of them goodnight and turned to go. Tino returned to his seat. Blanch immediately quizzed him, wanting to know who the man was. "That is Ernesto, a former lover of mine. He is in town for the launch party and wanted to make sure he and I would get along and avoid a scene."

Learning it wasn't Gabriel, Blanch settled back into her seat. She relaxed, rationalizing that she could not find a reason for Gabriel being in Monte Carlo. As she tuned back into Tino and Bobby's conversation, she caught the last part of the question her assistant had posed. Tino answered, "Ernesto is Lee's cousin from Madrid; that is how I met her."

Blanch spent the night tossing and turning in her bed. She rarely slept well when traveling these days; she preferred to be at home in her familiar surroundings. But it was something else bothering her this time; she couldn't get over the fact of how much Ernesto reminded her of Gabriel. It had been over thirty years since they parted ways, and the two times he corresponded with her were returned unopened. She wanted nothing further to do with him, then or now. That part of her life was long gone, and she preferred to leave it that way.

Finally falling asleep, she dreamt about the daughter she had forsaken. This was the first time she had ever dreamt about Kimberlee.

CHAPTER 20

Lee could not have been more pleased with the plans prepared for the launch of her new skincare line. There was a slight challenge with the seven-hour time difference between New York and Monaco but nothing that couldn't be overcome. The event planner scheduled Lee to speak at 10:00 PM in Monte Carlo; her presentation occurring at that hour resulted in the party in New York occurring late afternoon. Marketing had to convince the attendees in the US to dress in Black-Tie on a Saturday before five o'clock. Albeit not unheard of in the big apple, the event would need to last late into the evening to support the request of the attendees.

Knowing these two markets had such a large time difference, Lee opted to eliminate reciprocal viewing on the closed circuit broadcast. The primary location feed would be viewed at the secondary locations only.

Cameras followed her around the room as she mingled with her guests. The connections her husband and her father made during their life-times allowed her to entertain the whose who of the world. State leaders, congressmen from the states, and even a crown prince were in the mix.

Blanch arrived at the event alone as Bobby left her behind at the hotel, moving on to the event before she was ready. His phone calls to her room went unanswered as the phone by her bed was on DND. Even calls to her cell phone did not cause her to stir. She was in a very deep sleep. Thirty minutes before departure time from the hotel, she rang Bobby on his room phone. Explaining she had left her cell phone in her purse was why she had not heard it ring. Blanch agreed Bobby should go ahead and make the most of the party; she promised to arrive before Lee gave her speech.

The Versace gown Lee purchased for Blanch had been delivered to the hotel by Tino. When Blanch did not answer her door, a member of housekeeping accessed the room leaving the gift just inside the door. Looking stunning in the fitted evening gown, Blanch entered the event less confident than ever before. The dreams of the girl she birthed were troubling her psyche. Not knowing what had happened to her "sister," she had become somewhat distraught.

Assuming Kimberlee was living her life in Palestine, Texas, there had never been a desire on her part to reconnect until now. She was aware that Lydia was dead; her mother had been kind enough to leave her one hundred dollars when she passed. Blanch struggled to get the past out of her mind; the memories flooded her mind reducing her ability to work the room as she usually would have.

Searching the store's vast open space, she spotted Lee and made her way through the guests to her. The conversation was congratulatory and short; Lee was busy entertaining the prince. "Don't wander too far, my speech is scheduled for ten, and I don't want you to miss what I will say about Murrel International and you." The statement unsettled Blanch immensely; she did not want to be the focus of any attention this evening.

Recognizing the voice behind her, Blanch turned to find Bobby. She turned to join him and was surprised to see him holding Tino's hand. Something else new in her head to question; how long had this been going on? Migrating over to where they were standing, she averted her eyes away from their clenched hands, attempting to ignore the questions going through her mind. Tino motioned to the waiter to refill her empty glass.

Blanch had not eaten dinner and was hesitant to ingest her third glass of champagne, but she needed something to calm her jitters. The empty stemware was retrieved, and a fresh flute of Veuve was delivered, filled to the brim just as requested. Coming up for air after consuming half of the liquid in the crystal glass, Blanch saw Ernesto across the room. He was escorting Lee to the podium.

"Bonsoir, Buenas Noches, Guten Abend, Good Evening, Bienvenue." Ernesto greeted the guests, speaking their respective languages to bolster the international aspect of the business. He shared the exciting news of the party being broadcasted via satellite to each of the five stores, from New York to Madrid. Before introducing Lee, he noted she would deliver her speech in French, but her words would be translated on the monitors within each country. A large round of applause erupted in the room; this brilliant marketing move told the world this company was cutting edge in their technology as well as a global player.

As Lee began her ascent to the podium, Blanch leaned over to her companions, defiantly snarky as usual. "That's all great for the rest of the world, but for those of us here who are English speakers, how are we supposed to know what she says." In her usual snide way of condemning anything that made her lack control, her statement caused Bobby to giggle. Blanch was quick to squelch his outburst with her gaze; he knew the sideward glance and thought better about irritating her further.

"Is that the man you spoke to last night?" Blanch queried Tino while pointing to Ernesto. "Did you say she was his cousin?" Unaware his response would have such an impact, he confirmed her question. "Yes, Ernesto is her cousin; their fathers were brothers. It was fortunate Lee met the family shortly after Gabriel died."

The room was suddenly spinning for Blanch, the girl she was watching speak to hundreds of people was her child. Staring at the dark-complected woman, the spotlight was suddenly upon Blanch. Speaking in French, Lee acknowledged she was working with her mom, who currently owned a US manufacturing company. Blanch only understood the word 'maman'; she had no clue what else had been said. As the spotlight moved from Blanch, Lee smiled at her from the podium, a grin Blanch perceived as evil. As the beam of light returned to the beautiful woman on stage, Blanch felt a hand touch her shoulder. She turned to find Tessa Richards and Joanne Fergus beside her.

Unable to say a word, she began moving down the stairs to the main floor, searching for the doors that led out of the store. She had to escape as quickly as possible. She was running at full speed when she exited into the hilly streets of

Monte Carlo. The taxi driver never had a chance to apply his brakes before striking her with his car.

Lee was completely unaware of what had happened to Blanch until several minutes later when Bobby found her and shared the news. Immediately leaving the party, she asked her driver to take her to Centre Hospitalier Princesse Grace. This had never been a part of the plan for confronting her birth mother.

Convincing the hospital staff she was her daughter took some work. It wasn't until Bobby arrived with Blanch's passport that she was able to convince them; she knew every detail about her mother.

Blanch was conscious when Lee entered the room but could not speak as she had been intubated. The familiar red skin revealing her anger communicated all Lee needed to know. A nurse pulled the curtains closed, informing Lee a doctor would update her shortly. The doctor arrived a few moments later; his updates to Lee were in French. Blanch did not know what was said to

Lee; the panicked look in her eyes gave Lee the indicator necessary that she should translate for her mother.

Presenting the prognosis to Blanch as the doctor spoke, Lee omitted minute details she could not bring herself to say out loud. The doctor did not contradict what she said even though he caught the details left out of the translation. Blanch had a fifty-fifty chance of survival, but only if her spleen stopped bleeding. Lee, showing very little emotion, shared the chance for survival with Blanch.

Lee walked with the doctor from the partitioned area and thanked him for his efforts to save Blanch. He did not respond; he simply pulled her close and hugged her while she cried. She had not been in the arms of another man since Jacque had died; this was the warmth she needed to release the anger against Blanch Murrel.

Walking back into the curtained area where her mother lay, she found Blanch to be incoherent. Her pulse was low but appeared steady. A nurse entered, handing Lee a piece of paper. A note that had been written in Blanch's handwriting. Lee looked at the paper inquisitively; the nurse told how Blanch had reached for the pad in her pocket. Looking at her birth mother, she noticed the ballpoint Bic still in her hand.

Lee read the note before laying it by her mother's bedside. Blanch's words were typical of the woman who abandoned her back in Texas. She exited the room leaving the paper on the bedside tray. The two would never engage in a conversation again.

The doctor returned to find the crumpled paper in his patient's hand. Confirming she was deceased, he removed the tear-stained paper from the dead woman's hand before inappropriately reading what Blanch wrote to her child.

"I never wanted the burden of a child as I knew it would be too costly. Laying here in this bed is all the proof I need. I didn't want you interfering with my life then, and I don't want you in it now. I want to die in peace, alone. DO NOT hold any type of visitation for me; no funerals, no eulogies, nothing. I couldn't care less what the good-

byes from people I know would be, them or you."
The scrawled signature was simply a capital B.
The physician slid the note into his pocket while
thinking about the signature. He discerned the
capital B was an accurate description of the dead
woman lying on the gurney.

Lee sat on a bench outside the hospital
looking at the boats anchored in the harbor
across from the hospital. Hearing the bell ringing
from the nearby tower, she counted the chimes
six times. The sun was slowly peeking over the
horizon, illuminating the diamond brooch on her
lapel; she forgot she was still dressed to the nines
from the party the evening before.

She wasn't sure what to do next; she knew
Bobby and the team in Dallas had to be told of the
events that day, but she felt no urgency about
having that conversation. She was suddenly startled by a hot cup of coffee touching the edge of her
wrist; the doctor who had tended to her mother
asked if he might join her. Sliding to the left of the
bench, she indicated he should sit.

He revealed that his first purpose was to confirm she knew her mother had passed on. Pulling the note from his pocket, he handed it to Lee. "I found this in her hand. I assume you want to discard this on your terms. I didn't want anyone else to have it or the contents to wind up in a police file. I will have it shredded if you want." Lee looked up at the man and questioned why he was being so kind. "She was not a very nice person, but I am sorry for her de..." Lee stopped speaking mid-sentence, realizing how harsh she must have sounded.

The man confessed to reading the note before sharing his assumptions about her behavior. He continued on telling how he had been left on an orphanage door by a young girl who was fifteen years old. "I was fortunate as the family that adopted me gave me wonderful opportunities I would have never had without them. I met the woman who bore me once; she sought me out, seeking forgiveness for the choice she made."

Lee listened and wondered why he had such a positive attitude about his life and his being abandoned. All things considered, Blanch did right by her. Lydia raising her led her to the life she had now, which was more than she could have ever imagined. "How is it you don't have any negative emotion towards her?" Lee waited for his answer while he finished his cup of semi-cold caffeine. Reaching into his pocket, he retrieved his car keys and offered to drive her to wherever she needed to be. "I am done with my shift and would gladly take you wherever you want to go. I am sure there are people wondering where you are and the status of your mother." It was the first time she had ever heard anyone else refer to Blanch as her mother. Hearing the words, she thought they might sting her soul, but alas, she felt nothing. This was the release for her soul she needed; the tears she now shed were because she had no emotions for the person who had just lost their life.

Lee asked the doctor if he would drop her at Hôtel de Paris. She needed to speak with Bobby and assumed Tino would be with him. Handing the handwritten note back to the kind man who drove her to the hotel, she asked that he destroy it as she did not want that memory with her going forward. She thanked him for his kindness as the doorman opened her car door. The good doctor watched as she moved up the stairs toward the entrance of the hotel; he was impressed with her strength and grace.

Bobby opened the door to escort his companion from the previous evening to the elevator, only to find Lee standing there. She had not worked up the nerve to knock and was startled when the door opened unexpectedly. She was even more surprised to find the man kissing Bobby goodbye was not Tino.

Bobby stepped back before inviting her in, clearing the path for his friend to exit the room. Bobby informed Lee he would return shortly after seeing his guest out. Lee sat down in the desk chair and waited; it was the only place to sit in the room that was not occupied with some piece of garment. Now, she had two things to discuss with him. She recognized the gentleman with Bobby but couldn't place where she knew him from.

Bobby returned to the room and began picking up articles of clothing from around the room. "I was not expecting you, obviously." He piled all the bits and bobs he collected in a pile by the bathroom door. Taking a seat on the sofa, he questioned how Blanch was doing. Lee thought the question to be odd; in her mind, if he had been that concerned, he would have stayed at the hospital instead of bringing a man to his room to fuck. It was with that thought she recognized the man; he was the ambulance tech who was assisting Blanch at the hospital.

"She's dead." That was it; no long explanations were needed as far as she was concerned. All of these people betraying each other, taking what they could from their supposed friends, she had reached her limit. Bobby looked up at her in shock; he had been assured by the ambulance driver that she would be ok. He certainly was not prepared for her next question. "What's the deal between you and Tino? Are you two just fucking, or are you fucking everyone over?"

"As I am guessing my future employment depends on my answer, I should be completely up-front with you." Lee nodded her agreement and recommended he clear the air. He began telling of how Blanch had treated him so poorly over the years, and due to his size and over-the-top gay personality, he had never been able to find a job elsewhere that matched what she paid him, so he stayed. In the early years of their working together, he made the mistake of telling her confidential details about his lover, who was married. "You mean Garret." Bobby quickly looked at her. He mentally questioned how she knew about Garret. He told Lee how Blanch rewarded him for that intel and how it set in motion their agreement for him to seek information and route it back to her. "I was her little bitch, literally. I retrieved it, and she rewarded me. When you came into the picture, I decided I should protect myself, which is why I started feeding information to Tino. I watched her play her games with others for years, and you were the first worthy adversary. All makes sense now, knowing you are her daughter."

Those words cut more deeply than the words on her mother's note.

"What do you know about Sombre? Is Tino sharing information back with you as well?" Lee waited for Bobby's response but was interrupted by a banging on the door to the room. Both of them heard Tino shouting from the other side. Bobby opened the door. Tino barged in, shouting. "You will never believe what that cunt has done!" Bobby tried to stop him before he said too much; unfortunately, he saw Lee just as the word she hated most exited his mouth.

Lee looked both of the men over as she rose from her seat, preparing to leave. She did not speak to Tino; that bridge was burned and falling quickly into the river below. "Bobby, I need you to call the other members of the C-team and tell them the news about their CEO. Excuse me, their former CEO. I will be in Dallas next week and will fill everyone in on the future of the company." She pulled the door closed behind her. Walking down the hall, she could hear Tino shouting at Bobby; he wanted to know everything said to Lee. The elevator doors opened just as she approached; two hotel guards were on their way to Bobby's room. This type of behavior was not tolerated in the Hôtel de Paris.

Requesting a taxi to return her to her apartment, she wondered how she wound up in this mess. Thinking about how she would resolve it all and return to being herself, the next great epiphany happened for her. She realized she didn't really know herself, and that was where she should start. Fate had continually handed her blessing after blessing, followed by tragedy after tragedy. In her adult life, she had never been able to explore on her own to determine who she wanted to be. Recognizing that she loved what Sombre had created and what it represented, she admitted to herself it didn't represent who she was.

Lee decided her time should be spent discovering who she was and what brought her joy.

CHAPTER 21

Lee returned to Dallas to resolve concerns amongst staff and suppliers. When Blanch partnered with Lee and eliminated the equity investors, she insisted Lee have her shares willed back to Murrel in case of her passing. Lee's lawyers insisted Blanch do the same.

Now the sole owner of Murrel International, Lee immediately made arrangements for all cash in the business to be dispersed to the vendors who were past due in receiving payments. The company's executives did not like the path she was taking but were well aware there was nothing they could do to alter the new owner's mind. Staff dutifully followed her directions as they knew it was likely the most prudent way to protect their jobs.

Behind closed doors, she requested the CFO resign, and when he suggested he would not, she removed a folder lying on top of both sets of books. They were sitting on her desk directly in front of him. Looking him dead on, she inquired, "Which set of books should I use to pay our suppliers?" She forced him to acknowledge the impropriety he had participated in. He packed his personal effects and was gone within the hour.

The rest of the staff, including Bobby, would interview with Tessa, who was soon to be the owner and CEO of Fergus Manufacturing. Lee purposefully eliminated all the ready cash in the company, leaving it a target for bankruptcy. Murrel International would sell off its assets to avoid bankruptcy and then close its doors permanently. The sale of Fergus was privately funded and sold at a "reasonable" price. Tessa guaranteed to keep Sombre as a customer as part of the sale. With a bit of finagling by their lawyers, the transfer of ownership served as reparations for what Blanch had done to the young Tessa.

Lee returned to Palestine, Texas, to spend some time reflecting. She was at a loss of what to do when it came to Sombre. She loved what she had created and was thrilled with the chance to serve a market that had been ignored for generations, but she couldn't stop the nagging feeling she should be something more worthwhile.

Tessa ventured to Palestine to meet with Lee in the town where they both grew up. It was very different for both of them now. Handing Lee the keys to her parents' long-vacant home, she confessed she had never been able to convince herself to sell it. Even after her father died in prison, she continued to let it sit, still full of all the original furnishings. "I know it's silly that I never let it go. Garret and I talked about returning here and turning it into a B&B." She went on to comment how her new husband would never set foot out of Dallas.

The two women reminisced about how the town was when they were young and agreed it was still a nice place to live if you were the right people. Both of them, having traveled the world, knew there was so much more to mankind, good and bad. For the most part, the people in this quiet East Texas town lacked the opportunity to experience life beyond the borders of Texas, leaving them at a loss for what the rest of the world was like.

Lee spent her days rambling around the four thousand square foot house. Each day she would fill her time by focusing on removing a layer of dust from a room. The drop clothes covering the furniture were removed, revealing upholstery that had not aged. Whoever Tessa had hired to close up the house treated it with the care of a museum curator. Lee knew little about the place; she merely recalled it was empty after the death of the woman who lived there. The myriad of ghost stories she recalled from her fellow students back in high school did not concern her. Nothing had bothered Lee since her arrival, and she had noticed feeling like she was being protected. She assumed it was Lydia, but perhaps she had other guardian angels as well.

With cell phones and email becoming commonplace, she stayed in contact with the people in charge of Sombre every day of the workweek. The company was meeting expectations for sales and growth, Lee was content to hear this news, but it did not fulfill her.

An audit of the company found Tino was hiding money in a separate account, as she had suspected. During the discovery phase, it was determined checks in minute amounts were forged with her signature. The signature was good enough to pass for hers except for one minor flaw; there was an accent over the 'e' in de Leon, which was incorrect. Bobby was cleared of any participation; Tino was prosecuted and sent back to Spain, where he was incarcerated. They never determined who the other signature was from, but Lee had her suspicions.

Six months flew by with Lee living in Tessa's home. She grew to find solace in the small town and decided she wanted to remain. Friendships were developing, and she liked being back in her hometown. On one of Tessa's frequent visits, she was surprised when Lee sought to buy the property. After Lee explained why and shared her long-term plan, Tessa refused to sell it to her. Lee wasn't prepared to beg and was entirely surprised by Tessa's response.

Sitting across from Lee in the living room where Tessa had grown up, she began to cry. "Will you excuse me for a few minutes?" Lee was now more confused than ever, but she politely left the room. Heading for the kitchen to open a bottle of wine, her instincts told her they would need it for the conversation that was coming.

Pressing 'End' on her cell phone, Tessa walked through the dining room towards the kitchen, where Lee was uncorking the bottle of red. Her eyes were red and swollen from crying. Lee heard her coming towards the kitchen as she popped the cork from the bottle.

Entering the room, she said, "It's all settled then. We agree. Yes?" Lee couldn't figure out what precisely that phone call was about. Tessa continued on, "Wonderful, you have opened a bottle of wine. I think we should celebrate and make a toast." Lee was now totally confused about what was going on with Tessa; she thought to herself, Tessa must be bipolar. Tessa retrieved the bottle from Lee's hands. Pouring the deep red liquid with its smoky aroma mixed with plums into the two glasses, she handed one to Lee. Lifting the other into the air, she shouted out, "Salut!"

Knowing why Lee wanted the house, Tessa called Joanne Fergus to reveal the request to her cousin. After a short discussion, the two ladies agreed to support Lee's next quest. The house and land it sat on were given to Lee, free of charge, by the two women. The one stipulation between the three was that the home for pregnant teens must be named to honor Lydia. Lee was beside herself with the beautiful gift from her friends.

Never having kids of her own for whatever reason, she now had a purpose for her life. Along with a place to feel safe, the young women who would live in Lydia's Cottage would receive coun-seling to help them make choices that best served mother and child. Any child not wanted by the parent or a family member would be raised under Lee's supervision alongside her staff. Her focus was to do whatever possible to ensure no child ever felt unwanted. She felt raising a child who knows the truth of their origin, without shame or guilt for someone else's choices, would result in a functioning adult, free from the bonds of abandonment.

With the details in place, the home began a complete renovation. While the work was being done, Lee spent a large amount of time seeking the first position she wanted to fill, a staff psychologist. She insisted each person applying for house staff, gardeners, or anyone working in the home, be interviewed by the practitioner alongside her. At each interview, she and the psychologist made it known the importance of involving the residents in daily chores. Anyone who wanted to work there would have to adhere to the requirement. Lee had been raised washing her own clothes, cooking, baking, and mowing the lawn. In her own opinion, these skill sets taught her the value of work and how to figure things out on the fly. She wanted anyone living at Lydia's Cottage to have all the opportunities she did.

Staff finally in place allowed her free time to return to Paris and her skincare company. Her employees knew she was busy opening the girls' home in Texas and were curious how Lee would manage both commitments. Meeting with her advisors on her long-term plan, she felt confident what she had devised would provide for both Sombre and Lydia's Cottage well into the future. She revealed her vision to her executive team before making the announcement to her staff.

She knew once she told the office staff about the goal, press releases would have to be released immediately to minimize the rumors their founder had jumped ship. She was stepping down as CEO but would retain full ownership for the next ten years. At that time, ownership of the company would be passed to the employees. She was creating a culture where people felt valued and would commit to long-term employment. Beyond her exit, Sombre would split profits every year into three equal parts; the first third would be reinvested into the growth of the company, the second part would be paid out to employees in the form of equity pay, and the remaining third would fund the venture in Texas.

Delivering the message to the entire staff via teleconference, she remarked how proud she was of the future they were creating on all fronts. She allowed ten minutes of Q&A for the team members; only one person asked a question. How would she financially survive by giving all the profits away?

Without missing a beat, she explained the hope provided to the young women at the cottage was all she needed. "Money is just a thing; it can be counted, used for transactions, given away, and society absolutely needs it to function. But what I have learned is money is just an object, a tangible tool that cannot fulfill one's heart. The woman who raised me used to tell me 'not to covet what others had.' I didn't understand what she meant back then, but I now know what she was trying to tell me; if objects are more important than people, you will always be lost and alone."

Before returning to Texas, Lee did a whirlwind tour of the stores and took time to visit her father's family. Spending a week at Pozuelo de Laverde with Ernesto and his new love provided memories she would keep forever. The family constantly prodded her to find a man to take care of her. She reminded them she didn't need a man to take care of her; she would appreciate one sharing her life with her, but perhaps that was best served by the memory of Jacque.

Her last evening in Madrid was spent at dinner alone with Ernesto. They discussed Tino and the events leading up to his arrest. Ernesto shared with her how Tino called often and begged forgiveness for his transgressions, "I remind him it was his choice to defraud you and that I can't do a thing to help him." Lee hated how things had turned out with Tino and was sorry that he went to jail, but she was not the only one he was stealing from. "Did I tell you I found out who was forging the checks with him?" Ernesto shook his head no while leaning in close for Lee to share the news. "It was my own god damned mother. In going through her personal things, I found some of her correspondence. I found a note she had written me; the same little mark above the second 'e' was there. She should have studied foreign language accents if she was going to use them."

Her last stop in Europe was Monte Carlo. She wanted to visit the store and finalize the sale of her apartment there. It had been one of the few things she and Jacque owned together; selling it was part of her letting him go. The apartment in Paris was relinquished to his family but remained available for her use whenever time permitted a visit. Lee knew she would always carry Jacque in her heart and that it was time to move on. The Laverde Tia's had all been correct when they said she should let him rest. It was time.

She was finding herself, and for the first time she could recall, she had no regrets. The journey she had been on in her life was incredible, and she wanted to share these opportunities with young women who were lost and afraid. She decided to celebrate her last evening in Monte Carlo with a five-course meal at the Hermitage Monte-Carlo. The last time she had eaten there was with Jacque; she thought it a fitting goodbye.

Sitting at the table for one with a view over the water, she received several looks from people wondering who the elegant woman dining alone was. She felt akin to Miss Havisham for one brief moment; all that was missing were the cobwebs flowing from the candle on her table and a tattered dress.

Lee didn't know why she had picked the black Channel gown from her closet; she just remembered how much her husband admired her in it. The final accent to the dress was the brooch she wore to their wedding. "This is truly an evening of goodbyes." Lifting her glass for a sip, she heard a man beg her pardon. She giggled as she realized she was talking to herself out loud. She turned back over her shoulder to explain to the gentleman, not expecting to see who the man sitting there was.

"Good evening Madame de Leon; I hoped I would run into you someday." Lee responded, "You will forgive me. But I never said thank you for all you did when my mother died."

The man excused himself from his guest before moving to Lee's booth. Commenting on how amazing she looked, she chastised him for flirting with her while with another woman. "That's my cousin, silly girl. She is visiting, and I promised her an exquisite meal before she returned home."

The doctor who had rescued Lee the night Blanch died was once again sitting across from her; she began to feel self-conscious. "I still have the note, should you ever want it back. I couldn't bring myself to destroy it. I don't know why." Looking past her shoulder, he signaled to his dining companion for one more minute of time. "I need to go and take care of my cousin; she is leaving tomorrow morning on the train to Nice. May I see you afterward?" Lee told him she was also leaving the next day on the same train and would not return to Monte Carlo anytime soon. Standing up from the table, he asked where he might be able to find her in the future. "In Texas," was all she replied.

All by herself again, she wondered why the handsome man made her nervous. Concluding, it didn't matter as she was continuing on with her new quest the very next day. She finished her meal and requested the bill. The waiter informed her it had been paid for by the gentleman. "What gentleman?" she asked while looking around the room. "The man who was sitting with you, Docteur Guifant."

Leaving the establishment, she decided to walk back to her apartment. She wanted to soak up the sounds of the city before abandoning it. Arriving at her building, she made her way to the home she was leaving behind. Everything she was taking with her was packed and waiting in the foyer. She sold most of the furnishings and artwork to the new owners; there was no place for them in her new life. The suitcase on her bed was open and ready for her last few belongings. She walked around the rooms for one final check; she wanted to be sure she had collected the things she wanted to remember about her life here. Satisfied she had everything she needed, she showered and crawled into her bed to sleep.

Arriving at the train station, she retrieved her ticket for the train on its way to Nice. She had one simple bag to carry; the rest was being shipped to the States. Boarding the train, she made her way toward her first-class seat. Checking her seat number on the ticket to confirm she had a window seat, she became slightly annoyed to look up and see someone sitting in her assigned place. She stopped and took a deep breath reminding herself it was only a seat and the train was not full; if she wanted a window seat, she would just grab another. Continuing down the aisle, assessing where she might sit, she realized the man in her seat was Dr. Guifant. He stood and reached out for her travel case, placing it on the rack over her seat. He then waved his hand, gesturing for her to take her seat.

She felt like a schoolgirl, giggling when she spoke. "What are you doing here?" Settling in, she turned to find him sitting down next to her. "I have always wanted to see Texas."

CHAPTER 22

Preparing for the wedding while taking on her first boarder at the cottage kept Lee incredibly busy. She and her fiancé agreed he would stay in Texas and begin a practice in the small town where they would live.

Dr. Guy Guifant followed Lee from Monte Carlo to Palestine, Texas, for good. He had not expected to see the lush landscape of East Texas; he envisioned it to be flat and wide open. He thought Texas to look like it did in the TV show "Dallas." He was thrilled to see it wasn't like that at all and said the topography reminded him of where he had grown up in France.

The two had fallen in love the night Blanch Murrel died; all it took was time and a twelve-hour flight from Nice to Dallas for them to realize it.

Prior to the nuptials, Tessa and Joanne made their way to Palestine to meet the man Lee had brought home from Europe. They couldn't have been more impressed with anyone. He was kind and gracious, incredibly good-looking, and adored Lee for the work she was doing. Guy shared with the women interviewing him about his life with the adoptive mother who raised him, acknowledging how fortunate he had been. Being aware this was not the case for most children, he was thrilled to be a part of Lee's life and to support her endeavor.

The three women and one man sat at the kitchen table, sharing stories while consuming bottles of exquisite red wine. Lee excused herself to go and check on the teenage girl now living with them. Six months along and cast out by her father, she had found Lydia's Cottage by accident. Moving up the stairs, she heard the group being rowdy in the kitchen; she would ask them to settle down after completing the bed check.

Walking back into the kitchen, she asked the group what all the commotion was. It was simply a combination of wine and silly stories; they were enjoying themselves immensely. Lee kissed her fiancé on the lips and headed toward the wine cellar to collect another bottle. She was happy that her friends were visiting and even more thrilled they were in love with Guy just as she was.

Closing the door to the cellar and locking it behind her, she climbed the stairs to the kitchen only to find the group had abandoned her. Moving toward the noise she heard in the living room, she found the group standing around the piano, discussing the photos on top of it. Guy had a silver frame in his hands that contained a photo of Lydia and Blanch.

Joanne pointed to the young Blanch. "That's the one; that's the girl who stole my chair."

The End

This is the third novel written by Thadeus Park-
land. As a writer and producer, various formats
for his works are available through P1Press.co.

Other titles available through P1Press are:

Deathbed Confession: My Son Was A Stolen Baby

My Life Being A Sensitive

8 Things You Should Know To Launch A Product Line

Ready To Own A Salon? 10 Things You Should Know

P1Press

ISBN 979-8-9861673-4-3